TOO MANY BOYS

The phone rang, and when Nan picked it up she had a funny feeling she knew who was calling.

"I'm sorry about this afternoon," Bill began. "Maybe I should take a course in relating to girls or something. Nan, would you go out with me Friday night, to a movie or something? I won't even hold your hand. I promise."

Nan held the phone tightly. "Listen. I've got a boyfriend. I'm not going out with anyone, least of all you." She hung up before he could answer.

When the phone rang again, a few minutes later, she almost didn't pick it up. But she did.

"It's your favorite boy, Evan Felson. How about a date Saturday night? You know you can't resist me."

"Evan," Nan yelled into the phone, *"please go away!"*

Too Many Boys

Celia Dickenson

BANTAM BOOKS
TORONTO • NEW YORK • LONDON • SYDNEY • AUCKLAND

RL 5, IL age 11 and up

TOO MANY BOYS

A Bantam Book / October 1984

Cover photo by Pat Hill

ISBN 0-553-24355-1

Published simultaneously in the United States and Canada

Too Many Boys

Chapter One

Nan Whitman got out of the taxi in front of the large, old apartment house and took a deep breath. The August heat rose from the pavement and surrounded her, making her wipe away the trickle of perspiration that ran down her cheek.

"Isn't it wonderful?" she asked, closing her eyes and inhaling again. "Smell that glorious city air."

Her father shook his head in disbelief. "Glorious!" he said. "Ninety-three degrees, one hundred percent humidity, and the usual New York City pollution."

He leaned into the back of the cab and started dragging a large, overstuffed duffel bag through the door. "What do kids take to camp these days? When I was a boy, I went to

Boy Scout camp with a change of underwear, and that was it."

Nan patted the duffel bag and grinned. "It isn't what I took, it's what I'm bringing back. Being an assistant counselor means every kid in your cabin makes a present for you."

"Just what we need," Jake Whitman muttered as he and Nan walked into the building. He put his arm around Nan's shoulders. "I'm glad you're back, anyway. Your mother is, too. I should warn you she's giving a lesson to a beginner. So be prepared for sounds coming from that piano like you've never heard before."

They walked into the cool marble lobby. The apartment house had been built before World War II and had a shabby elegance that Nan loved. Joey, the elderly doorman, came over and patted Nan on the cheek. He had been the doorman since the Whitmans moved into the house when Nan was six. For ten years he had watched over her, picked her up when she fell, kept an eye on her when she first started crossing the street, and felt a paternal pride in her as she became the pretty girl she now was, with long, brown hair, brown eyes that were almost hazel and a tall, slim figure.

"Hey, Nannie, I'm glad you're back. Mac has been up and down a dozen times, watching

the cabs pull up. Guess he really missed you."
He winked and chuckled softly.

As Nan and her father got into the small elevator, Nan said, "What did he wink for? Honestly, you'd think I was twelve years old."

Jake Whitman pushed the button for the fifth floor. "That's just the way his generation reacts to young love."

Nan shrugged. "It's pretty silly."

At the fifth floor, the elevator door opened onto a small foyer. There were only two apartments off the elevator, and both doors opened at once. Nan looked at her mother, who was eagerly waiting for her in one doorway and her boyfriend, Mac, arms stretched out, in the other.

Nan hesitated for a moment. Then she called, "Hi, Mom, darling," to Kit Whitman and threw herself into Mac's arms. He hugged her tightly, bent his head, and kissed her with a sweetness that showed how much he loved her and had missed her.

Jake and Kit Whitman watched the embrace silently. "I just hate kids who are afraid to show their feelings in front of their parents," Kit Whitman finally said jokingly.

Jake Whitman put his arm around his wife's shoulders and said wryly to Nan, "Why

3

don't you fool around behind our backs like kids are supposed to?"

At last Nan and Mac broke apart, and Mac grinned at her parents. "Hi," he said sheepishly.

Nan went to her mother and put her arms around her. "I missed you, Mom. I really did."

"I missed you, too, Nan." She looked at her daughter closely. "I think you lost weight. Did they feed you well?"

Nan laughed. "Not good food, but lots of it. Hey, can Mac come for dinner?"

Mac shook his head quickly, and strands of light brown hair fell onto his forehead, almost hiding his warm brown eyes. "No, Nan. Let your parents have some time alone with you. I'll see you after dinner."

Mrs. Whitman shot Mac a look of gratitude. Nan knew her mother liked him and liked his sensitivity. But Nan also knew her mother wished she would date other boys and felt sixteen was too young to be seeing one person only, even though she had admitted to Nan that Mac was special.

As Nan went into her apartment, she turned back to Mac and waved goodbye. "See you later."

A soft breeze flowed through the Whitman apartment. The windows in the front of the apartment were wide open, and street noises drifted up—car horns beeping, kids playing, the bell of an ice-cream wagon ringing. Nan hadn't heard those sounds in eight weeks, and at once they made her feel at home.

As she started dragging the duffel bag toward her bedroom in the back of the apartment, she asked, "Where's Zoe?"

At that same moment, eleven-year-old Zoe Whitman appeared. She had short, brown hair with a small face that was full of intelligence and curiosity. She nodded at Nan, trying to remain cool, but clearly she was happy that her sister was home. "Hi."

Nan picked up Zoe's cue. "Hi," she answered just as casually. Then she went over and pulled Zoe into her arms and hugged her tightly. For a moment Zoe returned the hug, but then she resumed her cool attitude.

Nan finished dragging the duffel bag into her room, heaved it onto her bed, and sank into a chair with a sigh of relief. She looked around at her room, reacquainting herself with the brightly striped bedspread and curtains, the orange shag rug on the floor, the polished furniture, and the big bookcase.

More than anything, Nan liked to read, and the bookcase was evidence of that, with every shelf crammed and spilling over. Nan was happiest in the old library around the corner. As she stared at her bookcase, she felt peaceful—as if she were out of the world and yet part of what seemed most important. She had never told anyone, because she was afraid it would seem strange or old-fashioned, but she wanted to do some kind of library work when she got out of school.

Kit Whitman appeared at the door of the room and said, "We thought we'd have an early dinner tonight. You must be hungry after your trip."

Nan got up from the chair and stretched her slim, well-formed body. "Sure. I can always eat. Just let me wash my hands."

When she entered the dining room, she gasped. "Just what I've dreamed about!"

The dining room table was covered with an assortment of New York delicatessen goodies: thin-sliced corned beef, pastrami that gave off a rich, spicy aroma, and platters of tongue and roast beef and cheese. A large bowl of potato salad was next to one piled high with creamy coleslaw. The sight of dill pickles made Nan's mouth water. A basket overflowed with rye bread, and Mrs. Whitman laughed. "I didn't think you got much of this at Camp Opowee."

"That's for sure," Nan answered as she sat down in her usual place.

Her mother and father sat at the ends of the table, and Zoe sat opposite Nan. Nan made a huge sandwich, and as she reached for the potato salad, she saw her mother and father exchange a look she couldn't quite figure out. Her mother raised her eyebrows, and her father shook his head and shrugged quickly. Nan stared at them, a spoon suspended in her hand. When Jake Whitman's eyes met Nan's, he sat up straighter in his chair and said with a suspicious heartiness, "So, tell me all about camp."

It was the kind of remark her father never would have made unless he was very nervous about *something*.

Nan put the spoon down and asked with concern, "Is anything wrong?"

"Not at all," her father answered abruptly with a half smile.

"Tell them, Jake," Kit Whitman said firmly. "Now is the best time."

Nan's father wiped his mouth with his napkin and cleared his throat. "Well, you've heard me talk about Aunt Binnie. You know, she's really my aunt's aunt, not really *my* aunt. Her mother was—"

"Jake," Kit Whitman interrupted. "Get on with it."

"You're right," he replied. "Well, Binnie has left me some money. Not a huge amount, but enough so that added to what your mother and I have saved, I can leave my job at the newspaper for a couple of years and start writing full-time."

Nan jumped up and went to her father to hug him. "I think it's wonderful, Dad. You've worked on that paper long enough."

Jake Whitman untangled Nan's arms from around his neck. "There's more, Nan. Go sit down."

Nan hesitated and went back to her chair. Her father cleared his throat again. "Well, this means we're all going to have to cut back some. Your mother is going to teach extra courses at the music school. I'm going to stop playing tennis on private courts and do more of the housework so we won't need cleaning help."

Nan interrupted. "I can get some kind of job after school."

And Zoe said, "I can baby-sit now. I'm old enough."

Kit Whitman gazed out the dining room window and was silent. Then she looked at Nan and said, "Nan, you're going to have to

8

give up Hampton. We can't afford a private high school anymore."

Nan stared at her mother and then her father. "What are you saying? Where will I go to school?"

Jake Whitman said softly, "We've spoken to the principal and a few other people at York High. Normally you'd have to take an exam to get in, since it's one of the best public schools in the city, but they've agreed to take you on the strength of your grades at Hampton. It's got a wonderful reputation, Nannie. You'll be happy there."

Nan tried to stop the tears, but they streamed down her cheeks. "I don't want to go to York High. It's all the way downtown. And what about my friends? I don't know anyone there. I'll be all alone." She put her head down in her hands and sobbed loudly.

"You'll make new friends," her mother said.

"I don't *want* new friends," Nan cried. She raised her head to look at her mother. "Isn't it enough that Mac's going halfway across the country to college in a few weeks? Now I have to cope with this, too?"

Her father looked pained. "I know it isn't easy, but it has to be, Nannie."

Between sobs Nan asked, "What about a

scholarship at Hampton? Then I could stay there!"

Kit Whitman shook her head. "You have a partial scholarship already, and that's all they give."

Nan stood up. "I won't go. I just *won't*."

Nan's mother stood up, too. Her face was pale, but her voice was determined. "Yes, you will, Nan. Your father is going to have a chance to do what he wants."

Nan ran from the table and out the front door, slamming it behind her. She rang Mac's doorbell and kept her finger on the buzzer until Mrs. Pommers opened the door.

"I have to see Mac," Nan cried. She started for Mac's room when Mrs. Pommers took her arm.

"He's not here now, Nan. He'll be back in about an hour. What's wrong?"

"I have to leave Hampton School and go to York High. I know, you're like them." Nan jerked her head in the direction of her apartment. "You don't think it's so terrible."

Mrs. Pommers brushed the hair off Nan's face. "Well, I'm sure it's hard on you, but you'll live. That I guarantee."

"Oh, grown-ups," Nan cried. "Can I use your phone?"

Mrs. Pommers stepped out of Nan's way. "Be my guest."

Nan ran the three blocks to her friend Wendy's house and flung herself into Wendy's arms when she opened the door. "Welcome home," Wendy said. Nan pulled Wendy into the bedroom and poured out her anguish.

"I don't believe it," Wendy said. "How could they? Nan, I'll never *see* you. I mean, not to have you in all my classes. It's pitiful."

Nan wiped her red eyes and blew her nose. "I'm like a captive. I mean, there's nothing I can do. I'm at their mercy."

Later that night Nan curled up next to Mac on the couch in Mac's living room. His arm was around her, and her head was on his shoulder. Evening had cooled off the city, and a breeze smelling of the nearby river drifted through the softly lit room.

"I know what they think," Nan said sadly. "They think I'm a spoiled brat who doesn't care about her own father's happiness. But that isn't true. You know that, Mac."

Mac kissed the top of Nan's head. "I know, Nannie. I really do."

Nan hardly heard Mac's reassurances. "It's just that everything is changing. You're starting school in Chicago. It's too far for you to come home weekends, and I can't afford to visit. I'll hardly see you."

"I'll be home for Thanksgiving. That's not too far off." Mac took her hand and kissed it.

"It's not just that," Nan went on. "I want to be with my friends. With Wendy and Lorraine and Tammie. I don't *want* to be an outsider in a strange school."

"Come on, Nan. There'll be some other kids who will be starting, just like you. And I'll be in a new place, too."

Nan burrowed her head into Mac's shoulder. "I don't know, Macdonald Pommers. You make it sound almost bearable."

Mac stood up and pulled Nan close to him. "Listen, we have two weeks before I go off to college and you go to York. Let's enjoy them. Have as much fun as we can and not worry about school or parents or anything."

Nan smiled and felt a little less anxious about everything that was changing in her life. "It's a deal," she said and kissed Mac's cheek.

Nan and Mac spent the next two weeks doing all the things they loved to do in the city. They picnicked in Central Park and rode their bikes along the Hudson River. They went to a movie and ate buckets of popcorn, and when the movie was over, they stayed and saw it again. They took a boat ride around Manhattan and walked down Fifth Avenue looking at the glittering displays in the store windows. They played video games and ate in little delicatessens. They spent time with their friends, and at the ends of the days, they spent time by themselves. Even though they didn't discuss their upcoming separation, it hung over them all the remaining time they had together.

Their final night together, they went to a goodbye party their friends had given for Mac. Later they sat silently in Nan's living room. Nan cuddled deeper into Mac's arms and finally asked, "What's going to happen to us? You know, a couple can be madly in love, but if they're separated for a while, they can drift apart."

"That won't happen to us," Mac said firmly.

"What's so different about us?" Nan moved out of Mac's arms and looked into his face.

"I couldn't ever go out with another girl, Nan," Mac said softly. "So how can we drift apart?"

"And I couldn't look at another boy," Nan said.

"Then we just won't date other people. I only want you, Nannie."

Nan sighed loudly. "Our parents will have fits, but I don't want anyone but you. I'll write every few days, Mac. Will you?"

Mac laughed ruefully. "I'm a rotten letter writer, Nan. I can't pretend I'm good at it. But I *will* try. Really. Anyway, I'll call you every Sunday. That's even better than writing—hearing your voice."

Nan sank back into Mac's arms, and he leaned his chin against the top of her head. The faint smell of his after-shave made Nan draw in her breath. She wanted to remember it when he was away from her.

Mac's arms tightened around her, and he whispered, "You'll see, Nannie, we'll be fine. I couldn't *not* love you." He turned her face toward his and kissed her gently, then with more feeling.

As Mac got up to leave, Nan asked, "What time are you going?"

"Early," he answered. "My plane is at nine, so I have to be out of here by seven."

"I'll get up and kiss you goodbye," Nan whispered.

"No," Mac said, "don't. My parents will be around—it will be a real scene. I want to say goodbye now, while we're alone."

He held her close for a moment. "Goodbye, Nan. I'll miss you."

Tears ran down Nan's cheeks. She held Mac tightly. "I'll miss you, too. Always."

Then he was gone.

Chapter Two

In the morning Nan woke up just before seven. She went out to the front of her apartment and placed her head against the door. She could hear Mac and his parents talking as they waited for the elevator. She closed her eyes and lost herself in the sound of his voice. Then Nan heard the elevator door open and close after them, and there was silence.

When she turned away from the door, she saw Zoe standing in the hall watching her. Zoe's usually sparkling eyes were serious. "He'll be back, Nannie," she said.

"I know, Zoe. I only have to wait until Thanksgiving. That's not so long." But in her mind the time until Thanksgiving seemed like forever.

Nan went into her bedroom and sat on the

edge of the bed. Even though it was only seven o'clock, she knew she would never be able to go back to sleep. She took a deep breath, reached for the phone next to her bed, and dialed Wendy's number. She knew Wendy would be appalled at being awakened so early, but Nan had to talk to her.

"Hello?" Wendy's sleep-filled voice said huskily.

"Wendy," Nan said urgently, "I have to see you."

"What time is it?" Wendy asked, still half asleep.

"Almost seven-thirty."

"What!" Wendy yelled, now fully awake. "Seven-thirty on a Sunday morning? What's with you, Nan?"

"I'm sorry, Wendy. I just—I just . . ." Nan's voice trailed off.

"Hey, it's OK. I understand. Come on over, but tell the doorman not to ring up to announce you. And don't ring the front door bell or my mother will have fits."

Nan quickly pulled on a pair of old jeans and a tank top, then ran through the quiet Sunday streets to Wendy's building. The doorman was one whom Wendy knew, and he let her go up. When Nan got to Wendy's door, she knocked on it as quietly as she could. Wendy

16

opened the door. She was wearing baby-doll pajamas, and her blond hair fell over her face.

"Come into my room—quietly," Wendy whispered. "My mother is still sleeping."

When they got into Wendy's bedroom, Wendy crawled back into her bed, and Nan sat on the edge of a small armchair near the window.

"I feel terrible. I think I may die," Nan said.

"No, you won't," Wendy said with assurance. "Mac's not gone forever."

"It isn't just Mac's going," Nan said, tears beginning to trickle down her cheeks. "That's bad enough, but having to start a new school tomorrow, that's almost worse."

Wendy pulled the sheet up to her chin. "Who knows, it might not be so bad. Maybe you'll meet a great guy there."

Nan glared at Wendy and stood up. "Are you crazy? I don't want a guy. I have Mac. And we agreed not to date other people. He's going to write a lot and call a lot. I won't even look at another boy."

Wendy sat up in bed and looked at Nan with astonishment. "You mean that? You aren't going to date *at all*? That's nuts. You're a growing, healthy young girl, and you act as if you're married."

Nan moved to the edge of Wendy's bed. "Be

serious. Please. It isn't a boy I'm worried about meeting. It's girls. I won't know one girl at York. No one to eat with or meet after class or talk school stuff with or call at night to go over homework—like we've always done. I've always had you and Lorraine and Tammie."

Wendy looked at Nan with sympathy. "I know. It *is* tough. But you'll have all of us after school."

Nan shook her head. "It isn't the same."

At that moment Wendy's mother stuck her head into Wendy's room. "Nan, it's only eight o'clock. What are you doing here so early?"

"Mostly crying," Nan said.

"Oh," Mrs. Feathers said. "Well, dry your eyes, and I'll make us some breakfast. How about cornflakes?"

Wendy's parents were divorced, and Mrs. Feathers was a chemist. Cooking was not one of her strong points, and meals in the Featherses' house usually came out of boxes of some sort.

In the kitchen Wendy tried her best to make Nan happy. And although Nan appreciated her friend's efforts, she just didn't feel like smiling or laughing. At nine o'clock she realized that Mac's plane was taking off, and this brought a fresh round of tears. She knew that crying only made her feel more miserable, but she couldn't keep the tears back.

Finally, Wendy suggested a movie in the afternoon. "It's called *The Giant Green Cat*," she said. "I'm not sure what it's about, but it *must* be fun."

Nan had to smile. She promised herself not to cry any more about Mac. He wouldn't want her to be sad.

That night when Nan was in bed, she felt the warm September air lying heavy in her room. Yet her hands and feet were icy. She kept trying to picture herself walking into a strange school building, into strange classrooms with strange kids, and she shivered.

"Oh, Mac," she said into the darkness. "If you were here, it wouldn't be so bad."

She was frightened—more frightened than she could remember in a long time. The new school was only part of it. The other part was being without Mac. She had been going with him for so long that she couldn't imagine not having him around. She didn't like depending on Mac to make her life full. And she knew that with or without Mac she was still Nan Whitman, a whole person, with her own life. But all the same, she felt totally alone.

Chapter Three

The next morning Nan's alarm went off at seven-thirty. She sat up in bed, and a feeling of dread swept over her. That day would be the first day at her new school.

She dressed slowly, putting on a pair of new jeans and a polo shirt. She hoped to make some new friends, so she wanted to look her best. She brushed her long hair until it gleamed, smoothed a little gloss on her lips, and went into the dining room. Her mother was at the table, reading a newspaper.

"I made fresh orange juice. I know you like it."

Nan poured a glass from the pitcher on the counter but didn't say anything.

"Nan, please," her mother said. "Try to be more mature. Try to understand."

"You could have at least consulted me," Nan said bitterly.

"There wasn't time, and you were away," Kit Whitman said. "This is so important to your father. Please don't be angry."

"Where is Dad, anyway? I thought he was going to stay home to write the great American novel."

Mrs. Whitman brushed some crumbs into a small pile. "He isn't leaving his job until next week."

Nan sighed and got up. "I have to go. It's a *long* trip down to this great new school you're forcing me to go to. I'll probably get mugged on the subway, and then you'll be sorry."

Mrs. Whitman got up and faced Nan. "Oh, get lost," she said and began to walk out of the room. But she paused at the door and turned back to Nan. "It's not going to be as bad as you think," she said softly.

But as Nan walked through the entrance of York High, she said to herself, *It's not as bad as I thought, it's worse.*

The halls were filled with kids in couples and groups, all talking and laughing. The school was big and impersonal, and the walls were painted a nauseous shade of green. There seemed to be more students just on the ground floor than there were in all of Hampton School, and they all seemed to know one another. Nan followed the signs into the administrative office.

After she got her schedule and was assigned a homeroom, a senior girl showed her how to find her room. She looked at Nan and smiled. "Everyone has a first day, and everyone lives through it," she said cheerfully.

"I'm not so sure about that," Nan said. "The living through it, I mean."

Her homeroom had about thirty kids in it. They looked up at her as she came into the room, but no one said anything. The teacher, Ms. Collins, motioned for her to come in. As Nan handed her records to her, Ms. Collins announced, "This is Nan Whitman. She's a transfer student. Try to be civilized to her."

One or two girls smiled at her, and a few of the boys gave her a quick once-over. One boy whistled appreciatively.

"OK, Dennis," Ms. Collins said. "Enough of that. We all can see she's pretty. If you want to tell her, tell her, but don't whistle!"

The morning passed in a haze of loneliness. Nan wandered from class to class, feeling like a lost child. At lunchtime she went into the cafeteria and sat at an empty table. She tried to look busy and read while she ate, but she was painfully aware of the talking and laughing going on around her. She yearned for Wendy and for the small, almost pretty cafeteria at Hampton. York's lunchroom was large and green and ugly.

She had just finished the last of her milk and cake when she heard a shy voice ask, "Is this seat taken?"

Nan looked up to see a tall, slim girl standing at the table. "No, no," Nan shouted. "Sit down. Please."

The girl put her tray down across from Nan. "This seems to be about the only empty seat left," she said.

"I'm glad," Nan said. "I mean, that you're sitting here. I'm Nan Whitman."

"I'm Diana Schultz. It's my first day here."

"Mine, too," Nan said, smiling. "It's awful, isn't it?"

Diana nodded vigorously. "We've just moved to New York from Maine, and well—here I am."

"I live in the city. I've just transferred from a private school because my father is going to write a book," Nan said, looking at Diana. "He couldn't afford to send me to private school anymore."

"At least you're in the same city you've always lived in," Diana said pathetically. "I'm just miserable."

"Join the group," Nan said and patted Diana's hand.

They compared their schedules but didn't have any classes together. They did arrange to meet for lunch the following day. Diana lived downtown, so they couldn't even manage to go to school together.

Nan dragged herself through the afternoon, going to history and American literature and French. It was the same in every class. The girls weren't mean or nasty; they just seemed to have their own things going already. Although many of them gave Nan friendly smiles, they didn't go out of their way to talk to her or introduce themselves.

The next couple of weeks were more or less a repeat of the first day. Nan tried to be friendly to the girls in her classes, and they did talk to her some about assignments and exams; but she didn't feel as if she could count any of them as friends. Lunchtimes she ate with Diana, and while sometimes she would wave to a classmate and point to an empty seat at their table, the girl would smile and point to where she had already decided to eat.

Diana helped Nan feel a little less lonely, but she didn't seem to mind her lack of friends as much as Nan did. Diana was shy and passive and tended to let things happen *to* her rather than try to *make* things happen.

"Don't you feel out of things here?" Nan asked at lunch one day. "Look around. Practically everyone is with a group, except us. Doesn't it bother you?"

Diana took a bite out of her sandwich and then put it down. "Not really. We have each other, and I have friends in Maine that I write to. I guess eventually I'll make more friends here, too."

That night on the phone Nan told Wendy about her conversation with Diana. "Well," Wendy said, "you still have all of us. I mean, you're just as close to me and the rest of the kids as you were. At least you have us."

"I know," Nan agreed. "It's only in school that I feel so awful. There's no one to call at night and gossip about what happened in English class. The kind of crazy things you and Tammie and I used to talk about. I can't even talk to you about school anymore. I have no idea what's going on at Hampton."

When she got off the phone, Nan felt more alone than ever. She needed company and went into the living room. Her mother was lying on the couch, obviously involved with the book she was reading. "Where's Dad?" Nan asked.

"He's in the kitchen baking bread," her mother answered, looking up. "It smells wonderful, doesn't it?"

Mr. Whitman, working at home for the first time in his life, had discovered the joys of being a househusband. Between long sessions at his typewriter, he baked and cooked and helped with the laundry and cleaning.

Nan wandered into the kitchen and watched her father open the oven and peer in. "Almost finished," he said. "Tomorrow I'm going to try a chocolate mousse."

Nan made a small grimace. "We're all going to get fat as pigs now that you're home. Why don't you take up plumbing instead? The faucet in the bathroom has been leaking for a week."

"I'll get to that eventually," her father said. "Meanwhile, why don't you straighten up your room? I tried to go in there today, but I couldn't even find the floor."

Nan heaved a big sigh. "I don't believe this. It isn't enough that Mother is always on me about my room—now you, too. Don't you think you should just stick to your typewriter?"

Her father smiled and patted Nan's head. "A well-rounded man can do all sorts of things. I'm going to learn how to iron, too."

"Oh, nuts," Nan cried and went back out to the living room.

Mrs. Whitman put down her book and looked at Nan from head to toe. "You don't talk much about school, and I'm afraid to ask. Afraid you'll start that how-could-you-do-this-to-me routine."

Nan shrugged. "It's just terrible. Mostly because I can't meet any girls. They all just go their own ways, and all I get is a smile and a word or two. I hate it."

Her mother thought for a while. "Do *you* talk to *them*?"

"Sure," Nan answered. "But that doesn't get me far. I guess I'm doomed to be alone there." She stood up and moved toward the living room door. "I have to write to Mac. See you later."

In her room Nan sat at her desk and gazed at the blank piece of paper in front of her. She felt that no one really understood what she was feeling. Everyone seemed to treat her loneliness so casually. She wondered if what she was feeling was abnormal in some way, but she *knew* it wasn't. She just wanted to feel less alone.

Chapter Four

Since Mac had left, Nan and he had kept in touch just as they had planned. Mac called on Sundays; he wrote once or twice a week, even if it was just a postcard; Nan wrote every couple of days. She poured her heart out to him, and he responded lovingly, if a little less emotionally. Nan missed him so much, but she maintained a feeling of closeness to him, thinking about him and talking to Wendy about him—as much as she thought Wendy could stand.

It was only when Nan went into the library at school or in her neighborhood that she really felt at peace and happy. She forgot about missing Mac then, forgot about her isolation at York, and just felt contented.

Joyce Unger, the school librarian, became

aware of Nan's visits, and one afternoon she said, "You really look like you like it here. Most of the kids can't wait to get whatever book they have to get and take off. But you hover around. You look comfortable."

Nan looked at Ms. Unger. She was young and wore jeans and a silk shirt. She looked like she might understand what Nan was feeling, and before Nan knew it, she was telling her how she wanted to find some girlfriends.

Joyce Unger considered that matter for a moment. Then she said, "Ever thought of joining a club? They're starting late this year—just now, in fact. That's a good way to make friends. Anyway, what have you got to lose?"

"Not much, I guess," Nan replied. "That's a great idea. Thanks!"

At lunch the next day, Nan grabbed Diana's hand as soon as she got to their table. "I'm going to change our lives," she said.

"I don't know if I want my life changed that much," Diana said, unwrapping her sandwich.

"Of course you do. You just don't know it yet. *We* are going to join a club."

Diana shook her head. "Not me. Anyway, what for?"

"Because," Nan answered, "Ms. Unger said

that's the way to make friends here. Of course, she's right."

"What club are you going to join?" Diana asked skeptically.

"I have to think about that." Nan pushed the food around on her plate. "I'm not really very good at much except reading, so it's a problem. But there are so many clubs—I'm sure I'll find something."

"You're on your own," Diana said.

"Just wait!" Nan replied, taking a forkful of rice. "When I tell you how many new people I've met, you'll change your mind."

At the dinner table that night, Nan announced that she was going to join the hiking club at school.

"Why?" Kit Whitman asked with surprise.

"The librarian told me joining a club is a good way to make friends, and that's what I want to do—make friends."

Her father pushed his chair a little bit away from the table and wiped his mouth. "How does a city school arrange a hiking club?"

Nan answered rapidly. "I'll find that out. All I know is I checked out what clubs York has, and the hiking club seems best for me."

Zoe giggled. "But you hate anything athletic. The only things you like to do at camp are things you can do indoors."

"I know," Nan answered. "But hiking is just like walking, right? And I love walking around the city. So that seems the most logical club to join. How can I go wrong?"

"I'm sure there's a way." Zoe ran out of the room before Nan could reply.

The first meeting of the hiking club was two days later after school. When Nan walked into the classroom where the club was getting together, she gave the group a quick once-over and breathed a sigh of relief. Counting quickly, she saw twelve hikers—seven girls and five boys. They looked up when she came in the room, a couple of them smiled, and one boy winked at her. Nan gave him a scathing look and sat down next to a small, blond girl.

The leader of the club was Mr. Callaway, who sat on his desk in front of the classroom. He was young and wore chinos and a sport jacket with suede patches at the elbows. He looked like he *should* be the leader of a hiking club—sturdy and intelligent.

"OK, gang," he began. "I see a few of you from last year and a few newcomers. So, I'll go over the ground rules and hiking basics for you new members."

He took off his jacket and threw it over a chair. "Our first hike will be next Saturday. We always hike on a weekend so that we have plenty of time. This first one will be easy so that you all get adjusted. We'll be going up near Croton, which is about an hour away. There are woods there that have good, well-marked trails, which should be reassuring to you all."

A boy in the back of the room asked, "How are we getting up there?"

Mr. Callaway leaned against the edge of the desk. "We'll have two station wagons that are being lent to me. I'll take one group, and Carol Wilson will take the second group. Ms. Wilson is a French teacher here; she's also my girlfriend."

The group laughed, and Nan felt an easing of tension. She looked around the room as nonchalantly as she could, and she liked the way the girls looked. They seemed friendly enough and casual. The boy who had winked at her smiled when their eyes met. She looked away quickly and then turned back to him and glared.

Mr. Callaway opened a notebook. "I'm going to mention a few essentials for you new hikers. Please, do as I say! It's for your own good. First of all, you should only hike with a buddy. *Never* go off by yourself. Stick to your partner, no matter what."

Nan liked that and looked around the room, trying to decide which girl she would ask to buddy with her. The winker pointed to himself when she looked at him. She vigorously shook her head no.

Mr. Callaway continued. "Wear good, comfortable walking shoes. Never wear shoes you haven't broken in. Dress for the weather. If it's hot, wear loose, lightweight clothes. But always take a sweater. The weather can change, and you'll freeze. If it's cool, wear layers of clothes you can take off and add to. Oh, and always bring a canteen of water. You can get very thirsty hiking."

"What about food?" asked a girl near the back of the room.

"Bring energy snacks, but we'll eat lunch at a fast food place before we start hiking," Mr. Callaway said.

"I'll bring your snack," the winker said, looking right at Nan.

"No, thanks." She glanced at the girl next to her and shrugged her shoulders.

The girl looked sympathetic. "He comes on strong," she said, "but he's harmless." She smiled, and Nan smiled back at her gratefully.

"OK, group," Mr. Callaway finished. "As I

said, the first hike is Saturday. We'll all meet at the main entrance to York at ten. We take off at ten-fifteen promptly. Anyone not here by then gets left behind. So be on time." He reached for his jacket and slung it over his shoulder. "See you Saturday morning."

When the meeting broke up, Nan hovered near the blond girl she'd been sitting next to. She was about to say something when the boy who had winked at her came over.

"Hi. My name is Evan Felson. Don't worry, I'll show you all the ropes. Just stick with me."

"I'm not worried, and I can manage on my own," Nan said curtly and turned to talk to the blond girl. She had moved away, however, and was across the room laughing with two other girls. Nan stared at them wistfully.

Evan Felson tapped her on the shoulder. "How about a Coke?" He smiled warmly, and Nan had to admit that when he smiled he was attractive. He was tall and athletic-looking with straight black hair and blue eyes.

Nan thought of Mac, and her heart seemed to wrench slightly. A wave of missing him swept over her, and she felt tears come to her eyes.

"Sorry, Evan. I have to get home." She

walked away quickly, leaving him staring after her, smiling.

"See you Saturday," he called after her.

Oh, get lost, Nan told him silently.

Chapter Five

When Nan woke up on Saturday morning, she knew it was going to be an unusually warm day; the air was already heavy with humidity. She stretched and reached over to the table next to her bed. She picked up a postcard and smiled as she looked at it. It had come from Mac the day before. All it had on it was a heart that Mac had clumsily drawn, and written inside the heart was "Mac Loves Nan." He didn't write much at one time, but just the fact that he had sent the card made Nan feel good.

Zoe knocked on the door and, without waiting for an answer, came in. "You're going to be late," she said. "Get up."

Nan sat up in bed and stretched again.

"What are you going to wear?" Zoe asked.

"Hmm. I think those great new shorts I bought last week and that long-sleeved, striped T-shirt."

Zoe scowled at Nan and shook her head. "You can't wear shorts on a hike. You'll get all scratched up. And you'll die of the heat in a long-sleeved anything. This trip is going to be a disaster. I just know it."

"Thanks, Mother," Nan said, watching Zoe taking some things out of the closet.

"Here." Zoe threw a lightweight pair of pants and a short-sleeved cotton shirt at Nan. "These should be comfortable. What shoes?"

Nan leaned down and began looking under the bed, coming up with a pair of scruffy sneakers. "These are just right."

"No!" Zoe shouted. "They're all wrong. They have no support. They're too flimsy. You need walking or running shoes."

"*Me* with running shoes?" Nan laughed. "The sneakers are the closest I have to that, and they're very comfortable. That's what Mr. Callaway said to wear."

"Suit yourself," Zoe answered. "But don't say I didn't warn you."

When Nan got to York High, most of the kids from the hiking club were already there. She tied the sweater she'd brought around her waist, put her canteen over one shoulder, and looked around for the blond girl who had spoken to her at the meeting. When Nan saw her, she gathered all her courage and went over to her.

"Hi. I'm Nan Whitman. Could we buddy together?"

The girl smiled and said, "My name is Hope Wandowsky. I'm sorry, but I've already got a partner." When she saw how disappointed Nan looked, she reached out and touched her arm. "Wait until we get up to Croton. You'll find a buddy there." Hope looked over Nan's shoulder. "Maybe before."

Evan Felson was walking toward Nan. "Hey, how about hiking with me?"

Nan looked around and saw some of the other girls talking in groups. "I don't think so, Evan. Thanks anyway."

But Evan was determined. He sat next to Nan on the ride up to Croton. He sat next to her in the fast food place where they had hamburgers. He trailed after her constantly, keeping up a one-sided conversation.

When they finally got to the woods where they were going to hike, Mr. Callaway said, "OK. Everyone have a buddy?"

Nan looked around desperately, and Evan

took her hand and yelled out, "I do." Nan gave up and resigned herself to walking with Evan.

"OK," Mr. Callaway continued. "Stick with your partner. Don't go off the trail. This is an easy hike—four miles on a well-marked path. You'll be going into the woods for two miles and coming out for two. Meet here when you're finished."

The group started out moving at the same pace, but very quickly some were going faster and some slower. They spread out along the trail, and before long Evan and Nan were alone. Nan was surprised to find that she was enjoying herself. The air was fresh, and a cool breeze moved through the overhanging trees. The smell of the moist earth rose up with each step she took. She breathed deeply and smiled. Even Evan's running chatter didn't bother her.

The trail at the beginning was wide enough for them to walk side by side. As they trudged along, Evan reached for Nan's hand, but she pulled away from him.

"I don't have any awful skin disease," Evan said, grinning. "You *can* hold my hand."

Nan ignored him. She stepped up her pace and walked briskly, letting her arms swing at her sides. She held her head high and her shoulders back—for a while. Then, after about half an hour, she became aware of the growing heat. Perspiration ran down her cheeks and back. Her hair, which she had worn loose, clung to her face and felt heavy on her back. Her arms had scratches from the branches on the side of the path, and her feet hurt. She knew she was getting blisters on the backs of her heels, and through her light-weight sneakers she felt every stone and branch she stepped on. After another fifteen minutes, she stopped.

"I have to sit down," Nan said. She was breathing heavily as she collapsed against a tree. Heat and humidity rose up around her, and she felt even more uncomfortable than when she had been walking. Sinking to the ground, she eagerly opened her canteen. She took a sip and spat the water out. "Ugh," she said. "It's warm."

Even sat down next to her and wiped off the water dripping down her chin. "You look awful," he said admiringly.

Nan gave him a dirty look. "Thanks." She leaned back against the tree and closed her eyes. "How can just putting one foot in front of the other be so exhausting—and make your feet hurt so much?"

Evan looked thoughtful. "Listen. I know a shortcut. The trail loops around up ahead. We just go off this trail a little, and we'll be out of the woods in no time."

Nan looked at him suspiciously. "How short a cut?"

"It will save us at least a mile of walking."

Nan wiped her forehead and looked at Evan steadily. "Are you *sure* you know what you're doing?"

Evan looked hurt. "Of course I do. I'm not an idiot." He held out his hand to her. "Come on. You'll love me for this."

He pulled Nan up, and she walked wearily beside him, limping slightly. Her feet hurt more now than before the break. They walked for another twenty minutes, and then Nan stood still. "Are you *sure*?" she asked again.

Again Evan said, "Of course," but his voice didn't seem to have the same confidence this time.

After ten more minutes, the trail narrowed, and Nan limped slowly behind Evan, letting him hold branches out of her way. Finally she stopped again and glared at him. "We're lost, aren't we?"

Evan looked at her guiltily. "I think so."

Nan sank to the ground and stared up at him. "I'm not walking one more step. If we just stay still, someone will find us—won't they?"

Looking upset, Evan sat down beside her.

"Sure. Mr. Callaway will come after us." Then he reverted to his grinning self and reached for her hand. "What's so terrible? The two of us alone in the woods." He leered at her jokingly.

Nan pushed his hand away. "Look, I have a boyfriend. Understand? He's away at college, but I'm not dating you or anyone else. I'm not interested in dating, so keep away from me."

Evan reached for her hand again. "A guy away? Well, sooner or later you're going to want to go out, and I'll be here." Nan put both of her hands behind her back.

"You're the last one I'd want to go out with. You'd probably get lost walking down Broadway."

They sat in silence for a little while. "We'll probably die of starvation before anyone finds us," Nan said plaintively. "And it will all be your fault."

Evan reached into his pocket and took out a small box of raisins. "Here," he offered.

"I hate raisins," Nan said firmly. She scowled at him and turned away. But the nastier she got and the more irritated she became with him, the more Evan seemed determined to charm her.

He reached down and unlaced one of her

sneakers, sliding it off her foot. "Why were you limping?"

Nan winced as he pulled her sock off. "I was limping because my feet are one big blister. I will probably develop gangrene and die."

Evan gave a low whistle as he looked at the blister on the back of her heel. "That must hurt," he said softly.

Nan pushed him away. "Don't think you can get to my heart through my feet. You still got us into this mess, and I don't like you much."

Evan grinned at her. "You're nasty, but you're lively."

They sat against the trees for over an hour. Every now and then one of them would stand and yell for help. But there was no response.

It began to get cooler, and Nan put her sweater around her shoulders. "We *may* even get an early snow. Maybe I'll die of frostbite instead of gangrene."

Suddenly a voice came from a distance. "Ev-an. Na-a-an." It was Mr. Callaway.

Nan jumped to her feet. "Here! Mr. Callaway, here."

"Keep calling and stay where you are," the voice answered.

Nan and Evan took turns yelling, and then Mr. Callaway appeared with Hope Wandowsky. He looked at Nan and shook his head.

Nan looked down at herself. She was dirty, barefoot, and bedraggled. "How did this happen?" Mr. Callaway asked. "I told you to stay on the path."

Nan pointed a shaking finger at Evan. "Never let him buddy up with anyone. He's a menace!" she cried.

When she got home, Nan sat in a hot tub for over an hour, trying to soak away her aches and pains. When she came out of the bathroom and limped into the living room, she said to her family, "OK, so I'm not a hiker. I'll just have to try something else. What do you think about—"

The ringing of the phone interrupted her. She went into the foyer to answer it. "Hello?"

"Hi, Nan. Feeling better?" a male voice asked.

Nan knew it was Evan, but she was annoyed that he assumed she'd recognize his voice.

"Who is this?" she asked formally.

"It's Evan." He sounded put off. "Feel like a movie?"

"Evan, I told you I have a boyfriend, and I'm not dating. Anyway, you'd get lost on your way to the theater."

"Very funny," he answered. "You'll change your mind eventually. I'll just keep calling."

"I'll never change my mind," Nan said firmly and slammed the receiver down.

The day had been a total loss. She hadn't made *one* girlfriend. She was just as alone at York as she had been. And now Evan was pestering her, too.

She picked up the phone and dialed Wendy's number. She wanted to tell her about the whole grisly day. But when Mrs. Feathers answered, she said that Wendy had gone out for the day. Nan left a message, hung up the phone, and sighed deeply. She limped to her bedroom, still feeling sore and miserable.

Chapter Six

When Nan was talking to Mac that Sunday, she longed to be with him more than ever.

"I miss you so much, Mac," she said. "There's no fun here anymore. No you, no old school, no girlfriends at York except Diana."

"I miss you, too, Nan," Mac said. His voice sounded sincere. "Your sweet perfume, going together, kissing you."

After his call, Nan went into Zoe's room and sat down on her bed. She was silent for a few moments, thinking about Mac. Then she announced, "I've decided to try the photography club."

Zoe looked at Nan with surprise. "Why photography?"

Nan shrugged. "There should be lots of girls there. After all, think of all the famous women

47

photographers there have been. Dorothea Lange and Margaret Bourke-White and Diana Arbus. And I do fine with a Polaroid."

"There's a difference," Zoe said firmly.

"Nonsense. A camera is a camera," Nan said with assurance.

Zoe smiled. "We'll see." The photography club met for the first time on the following Tuesday. Nan tried to persuade Diana to come with her, but Diana wasn't interested. "I don't know one end of a camera from the other, and I don't care, either," she said.

When Nan got to the classroom where the meeting was, she was happy to see mostly girls. They were busy talking to one another, comparing cameras and discussing things they'd like to shoot. It hadn't occurred to Nan to bring a camera to the first club meeting, and she felt out of it from the start.

She smiled tentatively at a tall, dark-haired girl who was sitting alone. The girl smiled back, and Nan walked over to the seat beside her. As she sat down, the teacher in charge of the club came in and started talking. She was a small, red-haired woman who had a camera slung over one shoulder. She was wearing a bright green sweater that made her hair seem even redder. She smiled at the group of eight students and began speaking quickly.

"OK, kids. I'm Ms. Cohen. And for those of you who don't know, this"—she pointed, smiling—"is a camera. Absolutely essential to taking pictures."

She looked at Nan for a moment. "You do have a camera, don't you?"

"Oh, sure. I just didn't think to bring it today."

Ms. Cohen nodded. "The first assignment for all of you is to go out and take some pictures of something in the city you think is especially interesting. I'd suggest that you newcomers read *Photography for the Beginner* by Esson. It will help you get used to a lot of new words you'll be hearing, and so on. You should also get to know someone in the club who is familiar with picture taking and developing. That's a must. At meetings we'll talk about composition, analyze photographs you take, and teach you all the secrets of the darkroom. Any questions?"

"OK. For the rest of this afternoon, just get to know one another. We'll meet a week from today, same time, same place. Go out and take pictures of something in the city you think is special, and we'll take it from there."

Ms. Cohen left the front of the room and circulated, talking to the students one at a time. Nan looked over at the girl who had smiled at her, but she was busy loading her camera and didn't seem to be interested in talking to anyone. Across the room was a thin, blond boy with wide, blue eyes who sat by himself, looking shy and lonely. As Nan stared at him, he looked up and met her gaze. His fair skin blushed a deep pink. Nan felt sorry for him, and she smiled again. This time he got up and walked over to her.

He was still blushing as he said, "Hi. I'm Bill Gibbons. Are you new here?"

Nan nodded. "Yes, and I really don't know anything about cameras, I have to admit."

Bill looked down at the camera in his hands and said shyly, "Well, I know a little. If I can help you, I'd be glad to."

She knew how he felt. It was obvious he wanted to be talking to anyone, rather than just sitting or standing alone.

"I'd like that. How do I begin?" Nan asked, glancing around at the girls busy talking together and looking at one another's cameras. Bill seemed to gather a little more assurance. "Take some pictures tomorrow, and I'll meet you outside the darkroom on Thursday and show you a few things about developing them. OK?"

He was so eager, so uncomfortable, that Nan agreed.

The next day Nan went to the main branch of the public library after school. She had always loved the two large, white-stone lions that flanked the steps up to the library, and she had decided to take pictures of them. But before she began, she wandered into the library and walked through many of the reading rooms. As always she felt a peace, a happiness, descend over her in the silent rooms. She loved the quiet of the rooms and the dark wood tables with comfortable chairs pulled close to them. She even loved the smell, made up of books and papers and old furniture. When she looked at her watch, she realized she had spent over an hour just walking from room to room and sitting down in a few of them. She ran down the wide marble staircase and out of the library.

She had borrowed her father's camera and took a roll of pictures of the dignified lions. She felt she had done fairly well and was eager to have Bill help her develop them.

The next day she waited for him outside the darkroom. The minutes went by, and she had just about decided that he had been too shy to meet her when she saw him running down the hall. He reached her side and stood still, trying to catch his breath.

"Sorry, Nan, I got tied up. I was afraid you

might have gone." His face flushed as he spoke, and he never met her eyes.

"That's OK," Nan said.

"Come on, let's get started," he said, still gasping. He opened the door to the darkroom, and they went in. In total darkness Bill wound the film around a metal spool and placed it in the developing tank. Then, with the lights on, he carefully explained each step in the development process as he poured solutions into the tank. When they had hung the negatives up to dry, Bill said, "Now we just wait awhile. The next step is to print a contact sheet and to enlarge some of the pictures. But I think we should let that go until tomorrow. We'll just wait until you can get a good look at your negatives."

He moved closer to Nan and put his arm around her. "You really were nice to meet me. Most girls don't want to have much to do with me."

Nan moved a little away from him, trying to get out from under his arm, but he tightened his grip on her shoulder. Then suddenly he leaned over to kiss her. Nan pushed him away and grabbed hold of the doorknob. She pulled hard, but it didn't budge. She pulled again. Then she stared at Bill. "We're locked in."

He moved away from her. "That's impossible. This door never locks."

Nan pulled at the knob again, and suddenly it came off in her hand. She cried out with surprise and rage. Turning to Bill she said, "Now look what you made me do!"

Bill laughed and then covered his mouth when he saw the anger in Nan's eyes. "*I* didn't do it, you did. You just don't know your own strength."

Nan looked at the doorknob in her hand and then threw it on the floor. "Now what do we do?"

Bill shrugged. "With the red light on outside, no one will try to open the door."

"*What* red light?" Nan asked angrily.

"When you're working in the darkroom, a red light goes on outside the door so that no one will open it and let light in that would ruin the film."

"Oh, great. You mean we're really stuck in here?" She started yelling loudly, "Help! Open the door!"

Bill shook his head. "No one will be around here for at least an hour, until they start cleaning up." He moved closer to Nan again and reached for her hand.

Nan shrieked and grabbed a pair of tongs. She shook them at Bill. "If you come near me,

I'll—I'll—" She knew there wasn't much she could do at all.

She sat down on the floor with her back against a cabinet. "I can't believe you. You seemed so sweet and shy, and you're really a monster."

Bill looked at her miserably. "I'm not a monster. I just don't know how to get along with girls."

"Well," Nan said firmly, "believe me, *this* is not the way."

Bill huddled next to her and whispered, "Gee, Nan, I'm sorry. I didn't know we were going to get locked in." He reached for her hand again. "Will you ever go out with me now?"

Nan roughly pulled her hand away. "Sure, I'll go out with you. Out of this stupid darkroom!"

After about an hour, during which Nan grumbled and Bill looked ready to cry, Nan heard sounds outside. "Help!" she yelled. "Help! We're locked in here."

The door sprang open. A cleaning woman stood outside with a pail and mop. She looked at Bill with disgust. "Honestly, Bill Gibbons, are you at it again?"

Nan let her breath out in a loud *whoosh*. "Again? He does this deliberately?"

The woman laughed. "I'd say Bill tries to lock himself in this room with a pretty girl about once a month."

Nan spun around and glared at Bill. "You *are* a monster," she cried.

Bill shrugged and still looked miserable. "You pulled the knob off. Anyway, I just wanted to get to know you better."

Nan brushed her hair out of her eyes. "Do me a favor. Don't ever offer to help with anything else again—ever." She gathered her books and rushed out of the darkroom.

That night when the phone rang, Nan had a funny feeling that she knew who was calling.

"I'm sorry," Bill said. "I'm really harmless, Nan. Maybe I should take a course in relating to girls or something. Nan, would you go out with me Friday night, to a movie or something? I won't even hold your hand. I promise."

Nan held the phone tightly. "Listen. I've got a boyfriend. I'm not going out with anyone, least of all you." She hung up before he could answer.

When the phone rang again, a few minutes later, she almost didn't pick it up. But she did.

"It's your favorite boy, Evan Felson. How about a date Saturday night? You know you can't resist me."

"Evan," Nan yelled into the phone, *"go away!"* She slammed down the receiver.

After school the next day, Nan was sprawled on Wendy's bed, eating a handful of potato chips. "OK, so photography isn't the answer, either. If any of the girls at that club want to be friends, it isn't worth having to fend off Bill Gibbons. Anyway, I don't think I have any real talent for photography."

"I could have told you that before you started," Wendy said.

"Well, I'm not giving up," Nan said firmly. "People don't succeed immediately at everything they do. There are lots of other clubs. I'll just keep trying."

Wendy looked at Nan with admiration. "You sure have determination. I would just give up and make do."

Nan got up and walked to the window next to Wendy's bed. "I can't. I want to have a good time in school, and that means having friends. I'm not going to sit around feeling sorry for myself. I've got to try as hard as I can to get what I want."

But that same day when she came home from Wendy's, Nan was overwhelmed by a sense of loneliness. Her mother was in the living room, giving a totally untalented child a piano lesson. Zoe was at a friend's house. Nan's father had locked himself in the den, and she could hear his typewriter going. Nan thought of all the afternoons just like this when she had rung Mac's doorbell and had been welcomed with a smile and his outstretched arms. She went into her room and took his picture off the dresser. "Oh, Mac, why did you have to grow up and go to college?" she asked softly.

It had been a little more than a month since Mac had gone away. He had called every Sunday, and it was wonderful talking to him, but not like speaking to him when they were together. He sent funny notes and postcards, but there were few real letters, so Nan didn't really know what he was doing and thinking. *Can we stay close and as much in love so far apart?* she wondered.

Chapter Seven

That weekend Nan went to a party given by Lorraine Wolner, one of her friends from Hampton School. But even though she knew most of the people there and it was a fun party, Nan just couldn't make herself have a good time. With a sense of loss, she remembered bursting into parties with Mac, ready for fun. Now, it seemed ridiculous for her to be alone in New York and for Mac to be sitting somewhere in Chicago alone, too. It wasn't that she didn't enjoy her friends—she did—she just missed the magic that Mac brought to her life.

On Monday morning she got to school early and glanced into the library as she went by. Joyce Unger was busy organizing a display of books, and Nan went in and began to help her.

As she piled up the books, Nan said, "In theory your idea was good. If you join a club, you meet people. But in reality, it hasn't worked yet. I've been to hiking and photography, and I haven't met any girls. Besides, I didn't even enjoy the things I was doing."

Ms. Unger laughed softly. "It might help if you picked a club that interested you. I didn't mean that you should just throw yourself into anything."

Nan glanced around the room. "Is there a library club?" she asked.

"Sorry," Ms. Unger said. "Can't say there is."

When Nan left the library, she stopped and read the items on the bulletin board outside her homeroom. One announcement caught her eye immediately. "Next meeting of the Gourmet Club will be held on Thursday."

Maybe, she thought, *that's the answer*. There might be some girls there who would be friendly.

As she and Zoe washed the dishes that night, Nan asked, "What do you think of a gourmet club?"

Zoe looked up from putting dishes into the dishwasher. "Well, I really don't think about gourmet clubs much at all."

Nan glanced at Zoe with annoyance. "I

didn't mean it that way. I mean, I think I'm going to join the one at school."

"Do you like to cook?" Zoe asked.

"Not really," Nan said, handing Zoe some dishes. "But I love to eat. That counts for something. Doesn't it?"

Zoe shook her head. "Not much."

Nan thrust a dish into Zoe's hands and said angrily, "You're a very cynical girl." Then she walked out of the kitchen.

On Thursday Nan went to the gourmet club meeting, sure that she was going to make some new friends. The large room in which the club met had long counters along the walls divided into individual work spaces. There were two stove rings set into the counter of each work space and a small oven above each space, along with shelves of different ingredients. Nan looked around the room quickly and gasped. There were ten boys and two girls. The two girls were obviously close friends and were poring over a cookbook together. Nan was about to walk out of the room when a loud voice boomed, "Come on in. We're always glad to see new faces."

Nan turned to see a large, white-haired man wearing a tall chef's hat. "I'm Mr. O'Connell, chef, teacher, adviser, etcetera. And you are—?"

Nan knew she had to stay. "I'm Nan Whitman. I'm new at York, sort of." She smiled at the two girls, who had looked up. They smiled back and then returned to their cookbook.

"Well," Mr. O'Connell said, "take the work area next to Colin." He gestured in the direction of a tall boy with red hair. The boy raised his hand and motioned for Nan to join him. Nan sighed with resignation and walked over to him. Colin smiled warmly, and Mr. O'Connell began talking.

"Today we are going to make chocolate feathery pudding. It is a delicious dessert and not too difficult to prepare." He stopped and looked at Nan. "You do know how to cook, Nan. Right?"

Nan was about to say that she could broil hamburgers, but she stopped as she saw the two girls watching her expectantly. They seemed as if they would make good friends, and Nan didn't want to disappoint them. "Oh, sure," she answered. "I cook all the time."

Colin had spotted Nan's hesitation. He adjusted his apron and said, "I'll help you, so don't worry. I'm going to open a restaurant someday, and I'm quite expert." He smiled smugly.

"What kind of restaurant?" Nan asked.

"Oh, probably nouvelle cuisine," he replied even more smugly.

Nan wasn't sure she knew what nouvelle cuisine was, but she had no intention of admitting that to Colin.

"What else would one do?" she asked.

"OK, let's settle down," Mr. O'Connell said. "Now read the recipe carefully before you start. Work slowly. If you need help, ask for it. Don't ruin a wonderful dessert because you don't know what you're doing."

Nan stared at the recipe in front of her and felt a mounting panic. This was *not* the kind of chocolate pudding she knew about, in which you just stirred in some milk and dumped it into little cups. But she felt Colin's eyes on her and straightened her shoulders.

"Really, this is so simple," she said firmly. She tucked her long hair behind her ears, reached into a pocket and took out two barrettes, and fastened her hair back. Everybody in the room was busy, so Nan grabbed the first dish she saw.

"Wait," Colin said. "*This* is a measuring cup." He waved a glass cup in front of her. "*This* is what you need first."

Nan grabbed the cup out of his hand. "I know it's a measuring cup. Just stay out of my pudding, please."

She looked at her recipe again. "Preheat oven to 350°." That was easy enough. She turned on the oven and looked at Colin, trying to match his smug smile.

He applauded silently. Nan glared at him and went back to the recipe. "Sift 1 cup sugar." She found the sugar on the shelf, and the sifter and a bowl, and followed the directions. The sugar fell into the bowl. *This is simple*, Nan thought to herself.

She read on. "Beat one egg until light." She felt the panic starting to return. What was light? She broke the egg into another bowl. *It feels pretty light to begin with*, she thought. She began beating vigorously. She beat until her arm hurt. Then she felt Colin's hand on hers.

"That's enough. It's going to disappear completely."

Nan turned to him and pushed his hand away. "Look, you beat your way, and I'll beat mine. OK?"

Nan returned to the recipe. "Stir in sugar gradually," she read. She lifted the bowl with the sugar and tilted it over the egg bowl. There was a sudden gush, and all the sugar fell into the egg mixture. *Oh, well*, Nan thought, *what difference can it make if it goes in slowly or quickly? In is in.*

Nan watched Colin out of the corner of her eye. He was gently, slowly letting his sugar fall into the egg.

"How come there are so many more boys in this club than girls?" she asked him.

Colin put down his spoon. "Why, Nan, the great chefs of the world are *all* men. Surely you know that." He grinned condescendingly.

"You know *why* they are all men?" Nan asked, her eyes darkening with anger.

"Why?"

Nan waved a spoon at Colin. "Because they keep their wives, sisters, and mothers at home cooking for *them.*"

"So you're one of those, eh?"

"Yes!" Nan said through narrowed lips. She turned back to her feathery pudding, which gave no indication yet of being feathery.

Nan mixed the sugar and egg and continued reading the recipe. "Stir in 1 cup milk, 1 tbs. melted butter, and 1½ oz. melted chocolate." Nan put the butter in a pan and placed it on the gas stove ring. She looked over at the two girls. They were bending over their counter and laughing softly. Nan gazed at them until she was distracted by a sizzling sound. She looked into the saucepan and saw that the butter was smoking and had turned brown.

She quickly grabbed a pot holder and took the pan off the burner.

Colin actually giggled and said, "Good thinking. I'm surprised you remembered the pot holder."

Nan turned to him angrily and said, "Just bug off. I don't need or want your comments."

Colin shook his head. "Sure, I'm just trying to help. I like you. You're the kind of girl who interests me."

"You don't even know me." Nan went back to her pudding. "Sift 1½ cups all-purpose flour. Resift with ¼ tsp. salt and 1½ tsp. double-action baking powder."

"You know," she said to Colin, "cooking terminology is ridiculous. All-purpose flour, for example. How many purposes can there be for flour? And double-acting baking powder. What would happen if it were only single-acting?"

"Why did you join this club?" Colin asked. "You have about as much cooking ability as a two-year-old."

Nan was getting tired of following the recipe. She quickly combined all the ingredients and poured the mixture into little cups. She set the cups in a pan of water, as the recipe said, and put the pan into the oven so the puddings could steam for half an hour. As she waited, she sat on a stool and thought about Mac. Soon it would be Thanksgiving. He would be back for a few days, and things would seem more normal. She remembered every detail of his face. She thought about how it felt to be in his arms and how good his after-shave smelled. She had gotten to imagining his kissing her when she looked up to see smoke coming out of her oven. She grabbed the door and pulled it open to find her little cups of chocolate pudding smoldering. She had reset the oven temperature without thinking and set it much too high. Nan pulled the pan out and set it down on the counter.

Colin moved over to her and stared at the burned pudding. "You really are inept."

"I hate cooking," Nan snapped at him and ran out of the room.

Colin ran after her, waving a pot holder. "Hey, wait! I want your phone number. Nan! Can't we be friends?"

That night Nan had dinner at Diana's, and afterward they sat in her bedroom, doing homework and talking. Nan explained her latest effort to meet some more girls and began to laugh when she got to the part about the burned pudding. The afternoon seemed so silly now, but she still regretted not having met anyone she liked. And for a moment Nan wondered if Diana wasn't right when she said, "Sometimes you can't push things, Nan. You have to let them happen naturally."

But Nan still couldn't agree. "You mean I shouldn't try to make friends? You sound like Wendy. But I can't be like that. I *have* to feel I'm at least making an effort to get what I want." She curled up in her chair.

Diana ran her hand through her short hair and leaned back against the bed on which she was sitting. "We really are so different."

Nan nodded. "But you're a good friend. You know, I wouldn't have burned that pudding if only I watched my mother more when she cooks. Or even my father. He's always saying that I should keep him company when he's making his new concoctions. I just never was interested before." Suddenly she stopped talking, jumped up, and walked over to the bed. "If all the boys are in the gourmet club, where are the girls?"

Diana yawned. "Beats me."

Nan reached over and shook Diana slightly. "They're in shop, of course. That's the club to join. Come with me, Diana. Please."

"You've worn me down. OK, I'll go with you to this one. Why, though, I don't know."

68

Nan smiled broadly, her brown eyes shining. She was sure her new plan was perfect.

Diana reached over to the table next to her bed and took two apples out of a bowl. She threw one to Nan. "You know, if you keep this club bit up, you are going to have accumulated more boyfriends than anyone else in York. I bet Colin calls and Evan *and* Bill."

"They aren't boyfriends at all," Nan answered. "I don't go out with any of them. The only boy I'm interested in is Mac."

Zoe came into the bathroom as Nan was brushing her hair that night. "I'm going to try the shop club," Nan said. "*That's* where the girls will be."

Zoe stared at Nan with disbelief. "You don't even know how to hammer a nail. You're worse than Dad—almost. Mom and I always have to do that kind of thing. You know that."

"I'll learn," Nan said firmly.

She went back into her room and waited for what she knew was coming—the pattern had to hold. Fifteen minutes later Colin called.

"How about some homemade feathery pudding? I'll bring it over tomorrow night."

"I never want to see another feathery pudding as long as I live." Then she stopped. "How did you get my number? You don't even know where I live."

"I met Evan Felson after school. When I described the terrific girl I'd met, he said it was you. He gave me your number."

"Wasn't that nice of him," Nan said sarcastically. "Do you boys always share girls' phone numbers?"

"You sure are hot-tempered. But there must be *something* nice about you. That's what attracts me, you're a puzzle. So how about tomorrow night?"

"No," Nan said curtly and hung up.

Chapter Eight

The next day, as Nan walked to her usual lunch table, she noticed that Evan and Colin were sitting with Diana.

Even before she sat down, Evan said, "Colin and I decided we are going to share you, until you decide which one of us you want."

"What are you talking about—share me?" Nan slammed her books down on the table. "I don't want *either* of you."

Colin ignored her comment and said, "Look, it's Friday. Why don't the four of us go to a movie tonight?"

Diana hesitated, bringing a fork to her mouth. "What makes you think I want to share in this production?" She picked up her books and her sandwich and started to walk away from the table. "See you later, Nan."

Nan scooped up her things and glared at Colin and Evan. "Now look what you've done. You've hurt her feelings. You are such creeps!" She ran after Diana. "Wait for me!"

They found an empty table and put their books on it. When Nan came back from the line with a tray, she said, "The shop club meets on Tuesdays."

Diana laughed loudly. "You're really something. What do you know or care about shop?"

"I don't know anything about it, but I do care about making some friends. It's worth a try."

Nan put a napkin onto her lap and started winding spaghetti around a fork. "Don't forget—you said you'd come with me to this one, Diana."

"I've changed my mind. There isn't a cell in my body that calls out for shop. I'd be a total disaster." She shook her head as she spoke.

"You have to," Nan pleaded. "I don't want to do it alone again. Please."

After a few minutes of silent eating, Diana gave in. "OK, but only once. And I'm only doing it for you. I know I'm going to hate it." Suddenly Diana shot a look at her watch and stood up. "We're going to be late for class."

Nan jumped up, toppling her books to the floor. She bent down and knocked heads with someone crawling around on the floor. "Bill, what are you doing?"

Bill Gibbons put his hand to his head, rubbing hard. "I was just trying to help you pick up your books."

"Don't," Nan said. "Don't help me. Please."

"OK. OK." He stood up and watched Nan gather her books herself. "How about a movie tonight? I'll even pay."

Nan stood up, clutching her books in one arm and grabbing her tray with her free hand. "If I went with you, I'd pay for myself. But I'm not going." She walked away quickly.

After school Nan was still feeling unsettled and sad and wanted a few minutes alone with her mother. She went across town and waited for her outside the music school where she taught.

When Mrs. Whitman walked out of the school door, she smiled broadly at the sight of Nan sitting with her back against the wall of the building, reading. "Hi," she said. She poked Nan's leg with her foot.

Nan jumped up and kissed her mother's cheek. "I thought we could walk home together. We hardly ever have time alone anymore. Since Dad is doing so much housework, we don't even have the time we used to have when we did dishes together."

"I know," Kit Whitman said. "But I must admit I love having him do more around the house than he used to. He likes it, too."

Kit put her arm around Nan's shoulders. "You didn't come here to talk about your father, though, did you?"

"No." Nan sighed. "I just wanted some old-fashioned mother-daughter talk."

Kit raised her eyebrows. "What's the problem?"

Nan looked down at her worn sneakers. "I just can't seem to make any girlfriends. I do have Diana, and I don't mean to discount her, but you know me—I need a whole group. I feel so out of things. I almost cry when I see groups of girls walking together in the halls, eating together, or leaving school to go to someone's house to study together. I'm scared that I'm going to go through all the rest of high school wanting something I can't get."

Nan stopped and brushed the tears off her cheeks. Her mother put her arms around her and said softly, "I'm so sorry. I wish I could help you, but you certainly are trying."

Nan laughed. "Sure, and all I do is attract boys."

"Have you told Mac that you're besieged by

half the boys at York High?" Kit Whitman asked.

"No," Nan said, feeling a twinge of guilt. "I'm not going out with anyone. I can't help it if they keep calling me."

"I think you should," her mother said firmly.

"Help it?" Nan asked, surprised.

"No, silly. Go out with someone."

"But what about Mac?" Nan asked. "I love him."

Mrs. Whitman took her arm off Nan's shoulders and looked closely at her. "You're sixteen, Nannie. And you're missing a lot of fun. You don't have to stop loving Mac just because you go out with a boy from school."

Nan stopped walking. "I'm really shocked at you. You want me to cheat on Mac."

Her mother got annoyed. "You're not married to him, you know. I'm just saying that maybe you should go to a movie or a party with a boy. Did you ever think that you might meet some *girls* when you're at a party? That's as good a way to get to know people as any."

Nan walked ahead of her mother. "No. I'm going to join the shop club."

"You should take your father with you," Kit Whitman muttered, shaking her head.

The next day Wendy and Nan walked through the Metropolitan Museum of Art, doing more talking than looking. "Can you imagine my mother suggesting I date other boys?" Nan said. "It's almost immoral."

Wendy looked closely at a painting. "I agree with her. I told you that from the start. You're not accomplishing anything sitting home alone every weekend."

Nan and Wendy didn't argue often, but Nan was ready to now. "I'm not trying to *accomplish* anything. I just don't feel like going out with anyone. I go to all the parties the gang has. You know that."

"Sure you do. You put your body there, but you sit in a chair and think about Mac the entire night. I wonder if he's doing the same thing?"

Nan's voice got louder, and people nearby began to stare at the two girls. "Are you saying that Mac is dating other girls?"

Wendy's voice rose, too. "How do I know what he's doing? But if he isn't, he should be. He's eighteen. He should go out if he feels like it. Not be tied down to someone hundreds of miles away."

"I thought you were my friend," Nan said.

"I *am* your friend. That's why I'm telling you this. Think about it." Wendy gave Nan a hug.

"Don't be angry. Come on, let's go get an ice cream."

That night and all day Sunday, Nan thought about what Wendy had said. But it seemed impossible to take her advice—going out with another boy was just unappealing. Yet, she had to admit, she did feel more out of things and lonelier.

On Tuesday before she went to the shop club, Nan stopped in at the library. Joyce Unger was going through the card catalog, pulling out cards. "Hi, Nan. How's it going?"

"I'm trying the shop club today. I feel good vibes about it."

"Are you good at that sort of stuff?" Ms. Unger asked.

"I'll let you know tomorrow." Nan winked and walked out of the room.

She met Diana at her locker, and they walked downstairs to the basement and the shop room together. Inside, there were long workbenches covered with drills and saws, nails, hammers, and wood. There were also ten boys. The boys welcomed Nan and Diana loudly.

"Well," Diana said. "This may be interesting after all."

An older male teacher was running the club. He nodded at Diana and Nan and motioned to two empty places at a workbench near a muscular, athletic-looking boy. Nan took Diana by the hand and pulled her along.

The boy introduced himself. "I'm Dan Grey. Welcome."

"Nan Whitman," Nan said and then, pointing to Diana, "Diana Schultz."

"I guess you know what you're doing, or you wouldn't be here," Dan said.

Nan hesitated. "Well—not exactly."

"She wants to learn," Diana said quickly. "Me, too. This really looks fascinating."

Nan looked at Diana and was surprised to see that Diana meant it. She was already examining all the tools and reading the instructions for making things.

Diana grabbed Nan's hand. "Look. This is easy to make." She pointed to a sheet with diagrams. "It's a breadboard. And it's a good place for us to start."

Nan closed her eyes for a moment. "The only place that would be good for me to start is toward the door."

Dan had overheard. "Don't go," he said. "Diana is right. Even a kid could make a breadboard." He took a piece of wood and handed it to Nan.

Nan looked at the piece of wood listlessly. But Diana was eager. "Come on. You just pencil the shape of the breadboard onto your piece of wood. Then you cut it out and sand it. Easy, isn't it?"

"How come all this seems so easy to you, and it's appalling to me?" Nan asked.

Diana shrugged. "I don't know." She started tracing the breadboard shape onto the wood.

Dan Grey shouldered his way between the two girls. "You make your breadboard," he said to Diana, "and I'll help Nan."

Diana smiled at Nan. "OK with me."

Nan turned to Dan and said as calmly as she could, "Please let Diana help me. I'll do better with her, I know it. Look at her—she's wonderful."

Diana turned on a jigsaw and was competently cutting out the piece of wood. "Just do what I do," she said.

Nan watched Diana's breadboard emerge neatly, then tried the jigsaw herself. Her breadboard was ragged and misshapen. Next, Diana read the instructions carefully, then sandpapered the edges of the board. Nan did the same, but ran the sandpaper over her fingers every few strokes and winced.

"Poor thing," Dan said. "You just weren't meant for this. Let me take you away from it all."

"I wasn't meant for *you*, either," Nan said.

She watched Diana, who was drilling a hole in the handle of her breadboard. "What's that for?" Nan asked.

"To put a piece of string through, so that you can hang the board up," Diana answered, whistling as she drilled.

Nan reached for a power drill and plugged it into an outlet.

"Wait!" Dan shouted. "Not that one—there are three things in that outlet already."

Suddenly the room was plunged into darkness. The shop teacher yelled, "What's happened?"

"We overloaded an outlet," Dan called back. "Nan didn't know we had a limit."

"Great," the teacher said. "Someone feel their way out of here and get the janitor to change the fuse. The rest of you stay put. I don't want anyone tripping in the dark."

A boy got to the door and opened it, but the basement hall was dark, too, and there was a loud voice asking what had happened. Nan felt Dan's arm around her shoulder. "Don't feel bad. It could happen to anyone."

"Yeah," Nan answered, "but it didn't."

She felt the tears running down her cheeks, and she put her head on Dan's shoulder and wept. In the dark he pulled her toward him and tightened his arm. When Nan realized what he was doing, she pulled away. "Go away!" she shouted.

Nan turned to Diana and continued crying on her shoulder. For fifteen minutes the club stayed in the room, laughing and joking. For the same amount of time, Nan sniffled and mopped her face. Finally the lights came on.

Dan looked at Nan warmly. "You're even pretty when you cry."

"I've had it. *I have had it*!" Nan ran out of the room and slammed the door behind her.

Chapter Nine

"I'm through," Nan said to Wendy when they met over the weekend. "No more clubs. No more dumb boys pawing me. So Diana is the only girlfriend I have in school. I'm lucky to have her. She's wonderful. I'll just live my everyday life, and soon Mac will be home—and that's that!"

So when Nan wasn't in school or with her old friends, she read, dreamed about Mac, did her homework, and sulked.

One evening she went into the kitchen and sat down to watch her father trying to iron a shirt.

"I think this is beyond me," he said, pulling the plug out of the wall. "Some things I don't care about, and ironing is one of them."

"Good," Nan said. "I was afraid you might

turn out to be the perfect househusband."
She looked at her father and smiled wanly.

"You're unhappy, eh, Nannie? You miss Mac?"

Nan nodded. "Yes, but he'll be home soon."

"Right," her father said, "but only for a weekend. Then what?"

"You agree with Mother. You think I should date, too. Don't you?" Nan's voice rose in anger.

"I think you might have more fun if you did," Mr. Whitman answered.

"If you were Mac, would you like it if I went out with other boys?" Nan asked belligerently.

Her father thought for a moment. "I'd hate it. But what's the harm in going to a movie with one of the thousands of boys who keep calling you?"

"I hate them. That's why I don't want to go out with them. They're all creeps. None of them even compares with Mac." She stood up and left the kitchen.

On the way to her bedroom, Nan passed Zoe's room and looked in. Zoe was sitting at her desk, so Nan went in and threw herself on her sister's bed. Zoe had dozens of rocks of all sizes and shapes on the desk and was carefully painting designs on them.

"What *are* you doing?" Nan asked with annoyance.

Zoe didn't lift her head from her painting. "I'm painting rocks," she said.

"Why would you do *that*?"

"Because I like to," Zoe answered lightly. "You ought to try it."

Nan stood up and moved toward the door. "I can't think of anything more boring than painting rocks."

Zoe raised her head and looked at Nan. "I meant you should do something you *like* for a change."

Nan bit her lip. "Don't be so smart. You're only eleven years old."

Zoe shrugged. "I can't help it if I'm wise beyond my years." She smiled and started to paint again.

Zoe's advice echoed in Nan's head for the next week: *Do something you like for a change*. All the clubs she had joined, and none of them had paid off or seemed worthwhile.

Finally it was the Wednesday before Thanksgiving—and Mac was home! When Nan heard the elevator stop on their floor, she threw the door open and ran into his arms. He held her tight and kissed her fervently, and everything was wonderful again. Life was as it had been before he'd left.

That night her parents went to a movie with Zoe, and finally Nan and Mac were alone.

"I've missed you so much, Mac," Nan whispered as he held her. She told him about her attempts to find new friends, but didn't mention Evan or Bill or Colin or Dan. Mac listened carefully and seemed to sympathize with Nan and all she'd been through. When she was finished, he gave her a long kiss.

"Now tell me what you've been doing and thinking and feeling," Nan said. "Your letters were always so short, and phone conversations get so frantic. I feel out of touch with you. Tell me everything."

"It's all so wonderful, Nan, so different from high school," Mac began. "The classes, for example—well, we study things in more depth. There's more independent work. You don't have the feeling someone is checking up on you all the time. And the people are great. They come from all over the country. So you get a variety of people, all thinking in different ways."

Nan listened, and a coldness crept slowly over her. Mac was talking about a world still two years away for her. She forced herself to concentrate on what Mac was saying.

"The dorm is great, too. There's a lot of traffic in and out of everyone's room, but the guys leave you alone when you want to study. The food is awful, but next year I may get my own apartment with a few of the guys."

The growing excitement in Mac's voice told Nan how much he was enjoying his new world. A world she didn't fit into in any way. She clasped her hands tightly and bit her lip.

Suddenly Mac stopped talking, put a finger under her chin, and raised her face. "Now you, Nannie. Tell me more about you."

But it all seemed so childish to Nan. *High school must seem so boring to him,* she thought. She tried to think of amusing, interesting things to tell him, but she couldn't. It was only when they were kissing that she felt the coldness disappear and really felt at home with Mac.

Mrs. Whitman invited the Pommers for Thanksgiving dinner, knowing that Nan couldn't bear to be apart from Mac for a minute. It was a festive meal with more food than anyone could possibly eat, and laughter and good spirits. After dinner Mac and Nan went to the movies, feeling so much in the holiday spirit that they took Zoe with them. Mac held Nan's hand tightly throughout the movie, and the coldness she'd felt the night before seemed to be just a memory.

One of the Hampton gang had a huge party on Friday night, and when Nan walked in with Mac, the months of feeling out of things fell away. Mostly, there were students from Hampton at the party, but a couple of the boys had been in Mac's class and were back from college, too. Nan watched silently as the boys from college gravitated toward one another and began talking about classes, comparing dorms and food, and laughing warmly. The coldness came back to Nan. This time she felt as if she might never be warm again.

Suddenly Mac looked away from the boys he was with and noticed the fear in Nan's eyes. He went over to her immediately. "Come on, Nannie. Dance with me."

He put his arms around her and held her close. She put her face on his shoulder and closed her eyes. *It's the same as it always has been. It is*, she thought. But why did she feel so cold?

They spent the next night alone together. They went out to dinner and walked through the familiar neighborhood streets, stopping in at a small coffee shop for dessert. The air was brisk as they went back home, and their breath left steamy clouds in the air. Now the coldness was natural, and Nan welcomed it.

They sat in Nan's living room again, and it was just as it had been the night before Mac had first gone away to college. All they had were a couple of hours left to be together.

Nan huddled in Mac's arms. She realized neither one of them had asked if the other had gone out with anyone else. She yearned to know but was too afraid to ask.

"It's different, Mac," Nan said, almost unable to get the words out.

Mac tightened his arms around her. "No. No, it isn't. Everything is fine. It's just that we had so little time. Things aren't as easy as they used to be, but nothing is different."

Tears running down her cheeks, Nan looked up at Mac. "Do you mean it? Do you really believe that?"

Mac wiped her tears away. "I mean it."

Nan tried to smile. "When you come back for Christmas vacation, we'll have a couple of weeks. That will be better." Mac was silent, and Nan felt him stiffen. "You are coming home, aren't you?" she asked.

Mac stood up and walked over to the windows. "I only found out today. I was going to tell you. My folks are planning a big family reunion at my grandmother's in Los Angeles.

Everyone is going to be there. My brother and his wife and kids are coming. Everyone, Nan. I have to go."

Nan sat stiffly. "You don't *have* to. You *could* come here and let them all go to California without you."

Mac turned to face her. "I want to go, Nan. I feel I owe it to my parents. It's a big sacrifice for them, sending me to college for four years. I want to show that I appreciate it. If they want me in California, I should go. I thought you'd understand."

Nan felt numb. "I *do* understand, but I hate it."

Mac came back to the couch and scooped Nan into his arms again. "I'll get back for a weekend in February. Really, I will. Nan, please, nothing is wrong between us. You'll see."

The next day Mac was gone again. And Nan clung to his words, letting them echo in her mind and heart.

Then it was Monday, and she was back at York with the same problems she'd had before Thanksgiving. *Do something you like for a change.* Nan heard echoes of Zoe's voice as she walked past the library. She looked in and saw Joyce Unger sitting at the desk. Suddenly Nan was struck with an idea. Before she could change her mind, she walked in and said, "Do you need any kind of help in here?"

Ms. Unger looked up, startled. "Do I need help? I need more than you can imagine. But, Nan, I can't pay you anything. I have Adam every day for a couple of hours, and I manage to pay him a little out of my tiny budget. But that's all I can afford."

Nan said quickly, "I don't care about the money. I just want to work in the library. Let me, please."

"Let you? Nan, come as often as you like. You're more welcome than you could imagine."

Nan smiled, feeling happy for the first time in weeks. But suddenly a thought crossed her mind. "Who's Adam?" she asked.

Ms. Unger moved her head in the direction of a dark-haired, thin boy who was putting books on the shelves. "Adam Naylor. He's a senior and works here part-time. I'd die without him, probably."

Nan watched Adam work for a minute, but he never raised his head to look at her. *Good,* she thought. *I won't have any trouble with him.*

At first Nan went to the library just a couple of afternoons a week. But she liked the work, and soon she was going in every day. She quickly learned all the things that had to be done. Ms. Unger showed her a lot, and Adam showed her the rest. He was friendly and helpful, but he never gave the slightest sign of anything more than a friendly interest in her. Nan relaxed and enjoyed herself.

One night she went into Zoe's room, almost shyly. "I'm doing what you said I should do."

Zoe was puzzled. "What's that?"

"I'm doing something I like. I'm working in the library."

Zoe smiled. "Great."

Nan started to leave Zoe's room and then said softly, "Thanks. For the advice, that is."

Zoe looked at Nan, and her eyes widened in her small face. "Thanks for saying thanks."

For a moment it seemed as if they were the same age, not older and younger sisters.

And as the days passed, Nan felt that Mac was right. Nothing was different. He called more often and sent his silly postcards. Nan still wrote almost every day, trying to keep in close touch with him. *It is the same*, she thought. *Almost*.

Chapter Ten

At lunch one day, Nan said to Diana, "It's the first time in my life that I feel a boy isn't thinking about the next step."

Diana looked up from her sandwich. "What boy?"

"Adam Naylor. The guy in the library. He's nice and helpful, but he doesn't make me feel he wants to be anything but friendly."

"That's what you want, isn't it?" Diana asked.

"Of course. What more would I want?"

But despite what she'd told Diana, Nan was aware of Adam Naylor—and it seemed that Adam was aware of Nan. She walked around the library and felt his eyes on her. When she knew he was busy, she would watch him, and she liked the energetic way he moved. One day she looked up from the card catalog she was working on and met his gaze. For a long moment they looked at each other. Then he smiled a slow, lovely grin that made her smile back.

Another thing was happening in the library. The same girls who were in her classes and in the clubs she had joined came in, mostly to do research for papers. Nan was helpful, polite, friendly; but she no longer felt any desperate need to make them like her. She had given up the frantic search for friendship.

One day Hope Wandowsky, the girl from the hiking club, came in with another girl. Hope looked pale and frazzled. She introduced Nan to her friend, who looked as harried as Hope did. "Hi, Nan. Remember me? This is Pam Weinberg. We're in American lit together, and we each have to do a report on a twentieth-century writer. Naturally, neither of us has started it, and it's due next week!"

Nan laughed. "I know how that feels. Anyway, can I help? I'm good at research."

Pam grabbed Nan's arm. "My writer's Carson McCullers. I love her stuff, but I don't know much about her."

Hope added, "I've got John Steinbeck. And I've only read one of his books."

Nan took over. She directed the girls to the

material they needed, made suggestions for organizing their papers, and gave them moral support. They all worked together for the next few days until their reports were finished. Pam and Hope told their friends about Nan, and her reputation spread quickly. Soon the library was full of girls who worked with Nan.

Then one night, the phone rang, and a high, friendly voice said, "Hi, Nan. This is Pam Weinberg. Remember me?"

"Sure," Nan answered. "You're the girl who reads all the Carson McCullers."

"Right. I'm also the girl who would have stepped out the window if you hadn't helped me with my report." She laughed. "Listen, some kids are coming over Friday night for pizza. I'd like you to come—if you want to."

"Want to?" Nan repeated. "I'd love it."

"Around eight," Pam said. "Four-twenty West End Avenue. Oh, listen, there won't be any boys, just six or seven girls. OK?"

"You don't know how OK that is," Nan said.

Little by little, Nan became friendly with more girls and began having the kind of fun and closeness she had been looking for. There were calls at night about schoolwork and school gossip. There were movies together and sessions of serious talk. Diana became part of the group, too, and life was more fun for Nan.

She was able to laugh now when Bill or Colin or Evan came into the library to try to get her to go out with them. She always refused, but they kept coming back.

"You'll change your mind," Evan said. "And I'll be waiting for you."

Adam watched Nan with Evan one day and said, "Why don't you go out with him? He seems like a nice guy."

Nan hesitated, and then she surprised herself by not telling Adam about Mac. "I just don't want to. He's nice but too immature."

Adam gave Nan one of his slow smiles and went back to work. Nan tried to dim her awareness of him, but she couldn't. She knew when he was watching her, when he wasn't. She knew when he moved from one part of the library to another. Once she blushed when their hands accidentally touched while they were working. And she felt guilty about her response. If she loved Mac, why did she want Adam to notice her so much?

One Friday afternoon in mid-December, Nan dropped a pile of books, and Adam bent to help her pick them up. It was the final moment. They gazed at each other as they stooped on the floor, neither of them able to pull his or her eyes away. Finally Adam said, "Would you like to go to a movie tomorrow night? Or do you have a date?"

Nan cleared her throat. "I don't have a date—and I'd love to." *Forgive me, Mac*, she thought.

She didn't say anything to her family until they were having dinner the next night. Adam was picking her up at eight, so Nan knew she would have to break the news soon.

"A friend is coming by tonight. We're going to the movies."

Nan's mother smiled. "That's nice. Who is it? Wendy?"

"No," Nan said, cutting her steak. "His name is Adam. Adam Naylor."

There was total silence at the table as everyone stared at Nan. Finally Mrs. Whitman said quickly, "Oh. That's a nice name."

Nan stood up. "I don't want any discussions. Any comments. OK? I have a date, that's all."

She went into her room and picked up the picture of Mac from her dresser. *Please understand*, she thought. Then she put it down and looked in the mirror. She brushed her hair and put on some lip gloss and a little eye makeup. She wanted to look good, but not too good. She took a pair of snug jeans from her closet and a soft, red wool sweater.

When Adam came by, she quickly introduced him to her parents and led him to the door. She wondered if she was imagining it or if they seemed to be looking at Adam more closely than was usual for them. *Are they comparing him to Mac?* she wondered.

As Adam and Nan waited for the elevator, Adam asked, "Does she always do that?"

"Does who do what?"

"Does your sister look at all your dates that way?" Adam grinned.

All my dates? Nan thought, suddenly feeling guilty that she hadn't told Adam about Mac. "She's only eleven," she said out loud. "You have to take that into consideration."

When they went outside into the cold air, Adam took her hand. "Do you mind if we don't go to the movies?"

"No," Nan answered. "What do you want to do instead?"

Adam looked at Nan intently. "I don't want to waste time where we can't talk. I want us to get to know each other. There's a nice little coffeehouse near here on Columbus Avenue. It's noisy, but a friend's older brother owns it, and he's saving us a booth."

Nan took a deep breath. "Sure. That's fine."

They walked quickly through the wintry streets. It was just a little over a week before Christmas, and Christmas trees and pine wreaths were being sold in front of a number of stores. Some of the trees looked bedraggled already, but they were festive, and there was a wonderful smell of pine in the air. When they got to the coffeehouse, Adam pushed his way through the noisy crowd and waved to a man who motioned them to the back. There was an empty booth with a big reserved sign on the table.

"Stick with me, kid," Adam said to Nan, "and you'll get nothing but the best."

Nan smiled and slipped into the booth. Adam sat opposite her. "What do you want to drink or eat?"

Nan shrugged. The last thing she was interested in at the moment was eating or drinking. "A hot chocolate, I guess," she said.

When the waitress came over, Adam ordered a hot chocolate, and a coffee and a pastry for himself. Then he turned back to Nan and said over the noise of the jukebox, "What's your favorite color? Who is your favorite author? What kind of music do you like? What do you want to do tomorrow?"

Nan laughed. "Yellow. The Brontes—all of them. Jazz. And tomorrow I have to study."

Then they began talking. They covered everything, eagerly: their childhoods; their present; what they liked; what they hated. It was all so easy, so natural. There were no awkward moments or silences. And there didn't seem to be enough time to fit it all in. They forgot everything around them, the people, the music, the loud voices, and laughter.

"You seem so sure of yourself," Nan said. "Like you have it all planned. What you want, don't want. That kind of thing."

Adam took a sip of coffee. "If I'm going to be a doctor, I have to have it all planned. I have to work like a crazy person to get the money together to make it through college *and* medical school. That's why I'm in the library every day. My folks can't afford to do it alone."

Nan looked at Adam thoughtfully. "That's why you seem so together. Because you know what you want."

"And you?" Adam asked. "What do you want?"

Nan hesitated. She didn't tell most people. "I want to do some kind of library work." She waited for Adam to laugh.

"I thought you might. That's great." He took her hand. "I've watched you in the library. You look so happy there."

Nan sighed. "A lot of people think it sounds pretty boring."

"Not me," Adam said. "I think if that's what you want to do, that's what you should do."

Then they sat silently, just gazing at each other. Nan was sure Adam must be able to hear her heart beating loudly. His eyes seemed to darken as he looked into hers, and she smiled nervously. "Maybe we should go."

"Why?" Adam asked. "Are you afraid of what you're feeling?"

"It's just getting late." She sighed again. "Yes, I'm afraid, but not for the reasons you think."

Now was the time to tell him about Mac. She knew it. But she didn't. She just sat silently and looked at the gold flecks in Adam's dark eyes. The room seemed to be empty except for the two of them.

Adam stood up. "Come on. Let's get out of here."

He paid the check, and they walked out into the street. Columbus Avenue was filled with people going in and out of cafés and bars, looking in the store windows, and just walking. It had gotten colder, but the sky was clear, and there were even a few stars that could be seen, which was unusual for Manhattan. In the middle of the crowds, Adam put his hands on Nan's shoulders and bent his head and kissed her. His mouth was icy and warm at the same time. It was the gentlest kiss she had ever had. Nan put her hand on his face and felt the warmth of his skin through her glove.

They walked through the streets without saying a word. Nan didn't think about anything except how happy she felt. Mac was hundreds of miles away, and she left him there.

When they reached her house, she knew she couldn't ask him up to the apartment. Sitting in the living room and making small talk with her parents would ruin this special evening. They stopped a few yards from the entrance to her house, and Nan leaned against the building.

"Do you mind if I don't go upstairs with you?" Adam asked. "I don't want to talk to anyone but you."

"I know," Nan said.

Adam leaned toward her, and once again she felt the warmth and sweetness of his kiss. She reached up and put her arms around his neck, hardly aware she was doing it.

"Good night," she whispered after another soft kiss. She turned and ran into her lobby.

Her parents were in their room, and Nan

102

went into her bedroom and closed the door. She sank onto the bed without turning on the light and stared up at the ceiling. The lights of passing cars moved across it. Nan just lay there, her down jacket soft and warm under her back. The wool hat she was wearing slid onto her forehead, and she left it there.

"What is happening?" she whispered. "What is happening to me?"

She got up and took off her boots and jacket and lay down in bed once more with the rest of her clothes on. She pulled the blankets up around her neck. "Oh, Adam," she said to herself before falling asleep.

She woke up suddenly in the middle of the night and turned on the light. It was four o'clock. She stumbled out of bed and into the kitchen and poured a glass of milk. She sat at the kitchen table and tried to quiet the uneasy feeling in her stomach.

"Nan?" Her mother's voice shook her from her thoughts. "Did you *just* get home?"

"No, of course not. I've been here for hours."

Mrs. Whitman sat down at the table with Nan. "Do you always sleep in your hat and pants and sweater?"

"I was just too tired to get undressed." Nan's voice was low and weary. She looked at her mother and tried to joke. "Do you always sleep in those sexy flannel pajamas?"

Her mother laughed. "What's the matter, Nan? You look awful."

Nan sighed. "I don't want to talk about it, Mom. Please."

Her mother persisted. "One doesn't have to be very smart to know what's wrong. You went out with Adam, and you enjoyed yourself. Maybe he kissed you good night and you liked that, too. Now you're feeling guilty about Mac. Right?"

Nan was silent for a moment. "Why do you think that's wrong?"

"I saw the way you looked at him, even in your mad rush to get out of the apartment. Anyway, it's not exactly unusual."

"I'm not going to hurt Mac," Nan said firmly.

Kit Whitman took Nan's empty glass and placed it in the sink. "If you like this boy, Nannie, you can't ignore it. If you do ignore it, some other boy will turn up eventually whom you like, and you'll just have to face the problem again."

Nan got up quickly. "I'm going to bed." She kissed her mother's cheek as she went by her.

Nan slept restlessly the remainder of the night. When she got up early the next morning, however, she knew what she had to do.

She spent the afternoon with Wendy. They sat on a bench in Riverside Park facing the Hudson River. The wind blew fiercely, and gray clouds swept across the sky. Wendy huddled inside her coat.

"Why are we sitting here like fools? It's freezing."

"I need some fresh air to clear my head," Nan said.

"So tell me about last night," Wendy said. "What's he like?"

Nan stared straight ahead blankly. "He's wonderful—and I'm not going to see him again."

"Why not?" Wendy sounded exasperated.

"I don't want to hurt Mac. He's too dear, and he loves me."

Wendy turned to Nan. "I think you're nuts. I really do. Well, if you don't want him, maybe I'll wander into the library some day and see if I can interest him."

Nan glared at Wendy.

"Aha," Wendy said triumphantly. "You wouldn't like that, would you? Think about it."

Chapter Eleven

The next afternoon Nan's heart pounded as she walked into the library. She could think of nothing except seeing Adam again. She had hardly put one foot inside the room when he came over to her.

"Hi." He grinned the funny smile he had and waited for her to answer.

"Hi," she replied, dreading what she had to say.

"How about a Coke after we leave here?" Adam asked. He smiled again and didn't wait for her answer. "Saturday night was special. It was the best time I've ever had with anyone."

"Adam, I can't go out with you again," Nan said. It was best to get it over quickly.

"Why not?" he asked with amazement. "I thought you had a great time."

"That's why," Nan answered. "If I hadn't enjoyed it so much, I'd see you again."

"Are you crazy?" Adam asked.

Nan twisted the ring on her finger. "I have a boyfriend in college in Chicago. We promised we wouldn't date while he's away. I shouldn't have gone out with you at all."

The library was beginning to fill up with students, and Ms. Unger motioned to Nan and Adam to get to work.

Adam put a hand on Nan's arm as she turned away from him. "Have a Coke with me so we can talk about this. It's the least you can do."

Nan knew he was right. "OK," she said, "but I won't be able to stay long."

To make matters worse, Evan Felson came into the library that afternoon. The other boys—Bill, Colin, and Dan—had given up trying to date her, but Evan persisted.

He leaned over the desk as she was sorting through some index cards. "I hear you went out with Adam Naylor Saturday night, so you must be dating again. How about me?"

"How do you know I went out with Adam? What kind of place is this?"

Evan shrugged. "A friend saw you at a coffeehouse on Columbus Avenue. What's the big deal?"

"I don't want to go out with you," Nan said sharply. "I'm not dating."

"What's Adam? Your brother?"

"Please, Evan, go away. I'm not going to date Adam, either."

Evan was indomitable, as usual. "OK. But call me when you can't stand our being apart one more minute." He walked to the door, turned, and waved goodbye. Nan had to laugh. Despite his persistence, Evan was likable and took her rejections with good spirits.

Suddenly Nan felt Adam's eyes on her, and she looked over at him. He was frowning. *Now look what you've done*, thought Nan. *You didn't want to hurt Mac, but you're hurting Adam instead.*

When they left the library, Nan and Adam went across the street to a small luncheonette. It was crowded, so they sat in the one booth that was empty. Adam didn't even wait for her to settle in before he asked, "So what's wrong?"

Nan sighed. "I explained, Adam."

"That explanation wasn't any good. You can't be so in love with your boyfriend if we could have the kind of night we had." He thought for a moment. "You like me, don't you?"

Nan nodded.

"We have a good time together, don't we?" he went on.

She nodded again.

"We like a lot of the same things, feel the same way about things. Right?"

Nan just looked down at her hands, which were spread out on the table.

Adam's voice became soft. "I felt something very strong when we kissed. Didn't you?"

Nan looked up at him. Her eyes were moist with tears. "Yes," she whispered.

Adam reached over and took her hand. "Nan, you can't ignore what we feel about each other."

"Yes, I can," she answered. "I have to."

Adam persisted. "Do you think this guy in Chicago would still want you to be his girl-friend if he knew how you felt about me?"

Nan stood up. "I only went out with you once. I've known Mac and cared about him for years. I'm not going out with you again!"

Adam stood up, too, and glared at her. "I have to fall for a nut. The school is filled with nice girls, smart girls, pretty girls, and I have to pick you. You know what? *You're* not crazy. I am."

Nan threw some change down on the table for her Coke and walked out of the shop.

She was in a daze all the way home on the subway. She was barely aware of people pushing in and out, of the rattling of the train, and the strange combination of smells. When she got to her station, she shoved her way out of the car and walked the two blocks home.

Her mother was teaching a late class, and Zoe was in her room studying. Nan smelled food, so she figured that her father was in the kitchen making dinner. She wandered in and asked listlessly, "Can I help?"

Jake Whitman looked up from the salad he was making. "You can set the table." He glanced at her quickly. "Oh, by the way, Mac called. Said to tell you he was on his way to California and he'd call you from there."

Nan grabbed placemats and silver from a drawer. "This is going to be a *great* Christmas, just *great*. Mac won't be here. I'm short of cash, so I can't do much. And nobody is even having a party."

"Well, Adam seemed nice. He'll be around, won't he?"

Nan whirled around to face her father. "Look, don't try to fool me. I know Mother spoke to you about Adam. You two never keep anything from each other. Doesn't it make life dull?"

Her father smiled. "Not dull, honey, comfortable. There's a difference."

Nan sank into a chair at the kitchen table. "I wish *I* felt comfortable."

Her father started to slice a tomato. "It's still Christmas. It's a nice time of year if you make it nice. It's up to you."

"Now you're going to lecture me about being a good, smiling, happy girl."

"I'm not going to ask you to be a smiling girl. I *am* going to ask you not to be a drag around the rest of us. If you're miserable, I'm sorry, you know I am. But don't spoil Christmas for us."

Nan went over to her father and put a hand on his shoulder. "I'm sorry, Dad. I'll try. Really."

Christmas vacation started a few days later. Nan was grateful that she wouldn't have to see Adam during vacation. It would give her time to get her feelings under control. She missed Mac, but she kept busy seeing the girls she had become friends with at York and Wendy and Diana. There were some parties after all that Nan went to, and she even found she could enjoy herself. Mac called on Christmas Day, and she felt happier than ever to hear from him. And on New Year's Eve, Nan had a good time at a party that Pam Weinberg gave.

When she got home that night, she sat in her room and thought about the coming year. Mac was still planning to come home for a weekend in February. Working in the library filled her with pleasure, and it would be even better when she put Adam out of her head. She now had new friends in school as well as her old ones from Hampton. Life really was quite good. She was just about to go to bed when the phone rang. She picked it up quickly, knowing it was Mac.

"Hello," she said softly.

"I want to wish you a Happy New Year."

"Adam?" Nan asked.

"Yes. Did I wake you?"

Nan sat cross-legged on her bed. "No. Happy New Year to you, too."

Adam cleared his throat. "Look, Nan, I just want you to know I won't hassle you in the library. I mean, if you've made up your mind, I won't bother you. I don't want to spoil the place for you, and I can't afford to give up the job."

Nan felt tears in her eyes. "Adam, don't even think about giving up your job. *I* should leave before you do."

Adam laughed softly. "I guess we're both grown-up enough to keep working together. I mean, I'll leave you alone if that's what you want."

"Adam, thanks."

"Sure, sure," he said. "See you at school."

She hung up and slid down on the bed. Zoe appeared at the door. "Who was calling at this hour?"

Nan sat up. "You know, every day you sound more and more like Mother. Go to bed. It's none of your business."

"It wasn't Mac. I know that."

"How do you know that, smartie?" Nan asked.

"You sound different with Mac. More like you. It was probably that Adam guy because you sounded so romantic."

"Go to bed!"

Adam kept his word. He didn't bother Nan in the library. But when they had to work together, Nan sensed the tension. She tried to keep her hands from touching his, and it was obvious that Adam did, too. No matter how hard she tried to ignore it, the awful and wonderful awareness of each other was always there. Nan knew exactly where he was, as if he were sending off some kind of waves.

One day Joyce Unger said softly to Nan, "Why don't you and Adam just go somewhere for a few minutes and kiss a couple of times? The electricity between the two of you is going to cause a short circuit. I can't concentrate on my work. It's like being part of a teen movie."

Nan knew what she meant, but as the weeks went by, nothing changed.

One day Evan came in and sat at a table, pretending to work—he never seemed to give up. Whenever Nan happened to glance at him, he was looking at either her or Adam, adding one and one and coming up with two.

As Nan was leaving school to go home, Evan did, too. He fell into step beside her. "You like Adam, don't you?"

"Of course I like him. He's a very nice person," she said stiffly.

Evan snorted. "That's not what I mean. I mean *like*, really like."

Nan didn't say anything as they walked down the last couple of steps out of the building. "You haven't gone out with him again, my secret agents have informed me."

"You know, you're really unbelievable," Nan said.

"Why aren't you going out with him? He's nuts about you. I can tell."

"You know why I'm not going out with him. The same reason I wouldn't go out with you."

"Oh, yeah. That guy in Ohio."

115

"Chicago," Nan said.

"Whatever," he answered impatiently. "Listen. Let's go for a cup of coffee and talk about this. I can give you the male point of view."

Nan hesitated and studied Evan's face. He wasn't trying to ask her out. He was just interested. She didn't know why she agreed, but she did. "OK, but I have to call my parents and tell them I'll be late."

They went to the same luncheonette she and Adam had gone to a few weeks earlier. Nan found a pay phone near the cashier, and she dialed home.

Her father answered.

"Dad, I'll be a little late. I'm having a cup of coffee with Evan Felson."

"Another guy?" Mr. Whitman asked incredulously.

"It isn't what you think," Nan replied.

"I don't want to think any more at all. You're beyond figuring out. What time will you be home? I've made a wonderful stew."

"Around six-thirty. See you."

Evan ordered coffee for them. Before it was served, Nan was pouring out the whole story to him. How she felt about Adam. How he felt about her. How she felt about Mac. Everything.

Evan listened quietly. Then he said, "If I were that guy Matt—"

"Mac," Nan said.

"Whatever," he said again. "If I were Mac, I wouldn't want my girlfriend to keep going out with me just because she didn't want to hurt my feelings—when all the time she's nuts about some other guy. I'd hate that."

Just what Adam said, Nan thought.

"If I were Adam, I'd keep calling you. What's with him?"

"He respects my feelings," Nan answered.

"So he gets left out in the cold. You know, I sure don't understand women, but there are a lot of guys I don't understand, either."

Nan had to laugh. "Everyone isn't as persistent as you are." She looked at her watch. "It's late, Evan. I have to get home." She picked up her books and put down money for the coffee. "Thanks for talking to me. I liked it."

Evan looked Nan up and down. "You know, you're a cute girl. I'd have liked it if we could have gone out. But is there any reason why a guy and a girl can't be friends? I sure could use a woman to help me understand other women. And you're not doing so great in your relationships with guys. You could use a little help there, too."

Nan looked at Evan carefully. He meant it.

He wasn't trying to be devious. She smiled and said, "I'd like that, Evan. I really would."

After dinner that night, Nan was in her room doing her homework when Zoe came in and sat on the bed. "So who is this Evan guy?" she asked.

Nan didn't look up from her notebook. "He's just a friend. *Just* a friend."

Zoe perched on the edge of Nan's bed. "You sure have a lot of boyfriends."

"He isn't a boyfriend—he's a friend, period."

Zoe was silent for such a long time that finally Nan looked up at her. She was winding the fringe from a throw pillow around and around her finger. Finally she met Nan's gaze. "This boy in my class asked if he could walk me to Nina's party Friday night."

"Oh," Nan said.

Zoe ran her tongue across her lips. "I don't know if I want him to or not."

Nan now gave Zoe her complete attention. "Well, do other girls have boys walk them to parties?"

Zoe shrugged. "Some do, some don't. I just don't want to have to stay with him once I get there. You know, like it was a date or something weird like that?"

Nan left her chair and sat next to Zoe on the bed. "Do you like him?"

"He's OK, I guess. He's nice . . . smart—almost as smart as me."

Nan wasn't quite sure how to help Zoe, but finally she said, "I guess it can't hurt to have a boy walk you to a party. Can it?"

Zoe looked at Nan. "I don't know. I mean, one look at you, and I don't think this boy-girl stuff is so hot. Most of the time you just seem unhappy. Who needs that?"

Nan laughed. "It doesn't have to be like that. I mean, when Mac was here and we were together, it was nice. I wasn't unhappy then."

"Nan, is it Adam who's making you so sad?"

"I guess," Nan said softly. "In a way." Then she stood up and said firmly, "No! Of course not."

Zoe got up, too. "I think I'm going to tell this boy I'll walk to the party by myself. If I like him more by the end of the party, he can walk me home."

"You're smart, Zoe girl. You won't get into the kind of messes I do."

They smiled at each other. Then Zoe said, "I like it when we can talk like this—like grown-ups, sort of."

Nan said, "I like it, too."

Zoe hovered in the doorway. "Do you suppose this means we won't fight anymore and we'll always be able to talk together like we just did?"

Nan thought for a moment. "No, I think we'll still fight, but we'll also talk. Maybe that's what happens as we get older. I really like you, Zoe. You've got a good, clear head. I admire that."

Zoe looked startled. "No kidding?"

Nan laughed. "No kidding."

"Wow!" Zoe turned and ran out of the room.

Chapter Twelve

Nannie dear,

I'm a man of my word. I'll be home on Friday, February 24th. I'll fly out of here after my last class that day and be home that night. I'll have to leave early Sunday, but at least we'll have some time together.

I got some money from my family for Christmas, so it will pay for my ticket.

Everybody is back to work here. Vacation seems like it was a million years ago.

Have to study now. It won't be long until I see you, and I'll call you Sunday as usual.

Love and kisses,
Mac

Clutching the letter, Nan threw herself on

her bed. Relief flooded through her. Mac was coming home in less than a month, and everything would be all right again. She'd feel all the wonderful things she had felt for him, and once again Adam would just be the boy who worked in the library.

Which he wasn't now. Nan still had a painful awareness of him when they worked together. They were friendly toward each other, and polite, but that was all. Adam never tried to see her outside of school, and in the library it was obvious that he was doing his best not to look at her. And Nan tried as hard as she could to push the memories of the one date they'd had out of her head.

At lunch the next day, Evan sat at the table with Nan and Diana. Nan smiled broadly and announced, "I got a letter from Mac yesterday. He's coming home for a weekend at the end of February."

Diana nibbled on a carrot stick. "And what do you think that's going to solve?"

Evan nodded. "She's right," he agreed. "Diana is right. What do you think that's going to solve? So he'll be here for a weekend. Big deal."

Nan was surprised and annoyed by Evan's comments. "You know, I thought you were going to help me. Be supportive, like a friend should be. Instead, I hear the same kind of junk from you that I hear from Diana and Pam and my friends at Hampton. Who needs it?"

Evan inspected his sandwich carefully. "I wonder what this is." Then he looked at Nan. "I *am* being a friend. But friends aren't supposed to agree with everything you do. I'm just pointing out that Mac's coming home doesn't automatically change things for you. There is still Adam. Even if he *is* going out with Terry Collins some, he still likes you. I can tell."

Nan stopped pushing the tuna casserole around on her plate. "He's going out with Terry Collins?"

Diana and Evan exchanged glances. "Why shouldn't he?" Evan asked. "You won't go out with him."

Nan put her fork down. "Of course he should. Who said he shouldn't? I don't care if he takes out Princess Di."

"I don't think Prince Charles would like it," Diana said.

"Besides," Evan continued, "the princess is too old for him. Unless he goes for older women."

Diana took it from there. "Adam could *never* support her in the style to which she has become accustomed."

Evan tried to keep from laughing. "And she

123

has a child, too. I mean, he'd be saddled with a small prince right from the start. That is no way to begin a relationship."

The three of them burst out laughing, and Nan felt better. But the thought of Adam dating someone else still made her feel uneasy.

After lunch Diana went to her gym class, and Evan walked Nan to history.

"Diana is cute," he said.

Nan stopped walking. "Why do you boys think calling a girl 'cute' is a big compliment? Diana is intelligent, sensitive, warm, and attractive. What's the big deal about 'cute'?"

"OK, OK," Evan said. "She's intelligent, sensitive, warm, and attractive. Do you think she'd go out with me?"

"She's *too* intelligent for that," Nan said. Then she smiled. "Call her and find out."

Nan tore a sheet of paper out of her notebook, wrote Diana's number on it, and handed it to Evan. "You know, you have good taste."

"I liked you, didn't I?" he asked.

"I'm not so sure that's any indication of good taste, but liking Diana is. Good luck."

After classes Nan went to the library and started helping a girl who was doing a report on the French Revolution. Adam hadn't arrived yet, and Nan was aware that she was waiting for him. After half an hour she asked Joyce Unger where he was.

"He's home sick today," she replied.

Nan looked at the librarian anxiously. "What's wrong with him?"

Joyce Unger put her pencil down and examined Nan's face carefully. "He has a cold. But it's interesting how upset you got when you heard he wasn't feeling well."

"I like him. I'd get upset if you weren't feeling well, too."

Ms. Unger smiled and folded her arms. "But not quite as upset."

Nan ignored the last remark. "My boyfriend is coming home at the end of the month."

"That's nice. Do you think that's going to make you forget Adam?"

"There's nothing to remember!" Nan said curtly. "Everyone is making a big deal out of nothing."

That night Wendy came for dinner. At the table Nan said, "Maybe we should have a party or something for Mac when he gets home."

Wendy shook her head. "If he's only going to be here for two nights, he won't want to share you with a thousand other kids, will he?"

125

Nan shrugged. "I guess not. I just thought it might be fun."

"Sure, it would be fun," Wendy said, "but you certainly don't want to spend one of your precious nights at a party, do you?"

Nan looked at Wendy, who was questioning her with a slight smile that turned up the corners of her mouth.

Nan threw her napkin down on the table and got up. "Wendy, you can be a pain in the neck." She ran from the room and into her bedroom.

Wendy followed Nan and put her arm around her. "I'm sorry. I should have kept my mouth shut."

Nan sighed. "Why are all my friends giving me such a hard time? Don't you want me to love Mac?"

"I want you to love whomever you want and in whatever way you want. I just don't want you to fool yourself *or* Mac."

The week before Mac was due home it snowed. It started on a Friday afternoon, and when Nan left the library after five o'clock and walked out of York High, there was already a soft blanket on the steps of the school and the streets.

A voice behind her said, "It's beautiful. Isn't

it?" Nan turned to see Adam look up at the gently falling flakes and put out his tongue to catch some.

The city was almost dark already, except for the lights from buildings and on the street. The sky was filled with clouds, and it looked as if it might snow all night. But it wasn't too cold, and there was no wind. At once Nan noticed how silent and peaceful the streets had become. Most people had left their offices early. There were very few cars on the streets, and the normal city sounds were muffled by the blanket of white snow.

Nan felt the flakes gathering on her hair and on her eyelashes. She felt as though she were in a wonderful, magical world. As if he knew what she was feeling, Adam said, "With the snow in your hair, you look like a fairy princess."

Nan smiled. "Fairy princesses always have blond hair and blue eyes. I don't fit the type."

Adam smiled back at her. "Not my fairy princess. Since I was a kid, my princess had long, dark hair and brown eyes." He reached up and brushed some snowflakes off the top of her head.

She closed her eyes at his touch and let herself respond to it. He put his arm around her shoulders, and they walked together down the school steps. There seemed to be nothing in the whole world for Nan except Adam and the snow falling in the quiet night.

He reached down and picked up a handful of snow, molding it into a ball. He offered it to Nan solemnly. "For you, my princess. It is a magic snowball, and if you take it in your hand, you will forever be enchanted by the person who gives it to you."

Nan cupped her hands together, and Adam gently placed the snowball in them. "What happens when it melts?" she asked.

"Don't you know? Magic snowballs never melt."

Suddenly Adam said, "How much money do you have with you?"

Nan didn't question him. She took out her wallet and counted the bills. "Hmmm. Eleven dollars. My entire worldly goods."

Adam counted what he had. "I've got ten. If we pool our fortunes, I know a very bewitching Italian restaurant not far from here where we can have dinner." He waited almost without breathing for her answer.

For Nan, however, the rest of the world was unreal, and Adam was the only reality there was. "Lead on, my lord."

Holding hands, they walked through the streets. Every now and then Nan stopped and tilted her head back. She closed her eyes and let the snowflakes settle on her face. Once, as she did this, Adam bent over and kissed her. It was such a brief, soft kiss that Nan wasn't even sure it had happened.

When they got to the restaurant, Nan called her parents. Then the owner led them to a table in the half-filled semidarkness. The restaurant was tiny, and there were candles on all the tables. Red-checked tablecloths added to the picture-book look, and a fireplace with a blazing, crackling fire made everything perfect.

Nan and Adam had a wonderful dinner. There were steaming bowls of spaghetti, a loaf of crusty bread, salad, and delicious Italian sodas to drink. The restaurant was snug and warm, the ideal place to share a special meal. During dinner Adam laughed at Nan's efforts to wind the long strands of spaghetti around her fork, and once he reached over and wiped her chin, which was dripping with clam sauce. Afterward, over frothy cups of cappuccino, they sat and gazed at each other.

"Adam, listen—" Nan began.

Adam reached over and put a hand over her mouth. "Don't, Nan. Don't say a word. Let's just be happy now."

Nan nodded in agreement. Suddenly an old

woman came over to their table. "Would the young lady like to have her palm read?"

Adam quickly glanced at the check. "We won't have any money after we pay the bill. Sorry."

The woman looked at the two of them and smiled. "It's all right," she said. "The reading is a gift."

She pulled a chair up to the table, and Nan eagerly held out her hand. The woman peered at it in silence for a few minutes. Then she began in a melodic, almost hypnotic, voice. "I see a long life." She traced a line on Nan's palm. "And I see love, oh, lots of love." She glanced at Adam and smiled. Then she looked at Nan's palm again. "I see great success for you in whatever you do, and riches, too. Oh, yes, you will travel to far places, and you will be very happy." Then she stood up.

Adam said regretfully, "I wish we had some money to give you. That was a wonderful fortune."

The woman patted Nan's head and smiled at him. "That's all right. It was a pleasure to do."

On the way out, Nan went over to the palm reader, who was sitting at a table near the door. "Was that really what you saw in my palm?" she asked. "Am I really going to be happy?"

The woman nodded. "You will be as happy as you let yourself be. That is up to you."

On the street the snow had accumulated even more and was coming down more heavily. As Adam and Nan walked to the subway, they could hardly see in front of them. They would run up the street, each waiting for the other to follow. Each time Adam caught Nan or she caught him, they gave each other a snowy kiss.

Nan didn't think of Mac at all. He didn't seem to exist any more in the white night. On the subway Nan rested her head on Adam's shoulder as the train rocked uptown. A girl sitting across from Nan had her head on her boyfriend's shoulder, too, and she and Nan exchanged sleepy smiles.

When they reached Nan's stop, they got off the train and went once again into the snow-filled night. "Don't go home yet, Nan. Stay a little longer," Adam asked her.

"Where can we go? We don't have any money left."

There was a video arcade on the corner, and Adam took three quarters out of his pocket. He raised his eyebrows in a question, and Nan smiled in agreement. They went inside the small store and played three games. Then they watched some kids at other machines and yelled instructions to them. When they finally left, they were filled with energy again and ran down the street, throwing snowballs at each other.

At her house Nan hesitated, but then she asked, "Would you like to come up for a hot chocolate or something?"

"Sure. If it's OK."

Nan's parents were in the living room, and Nan and Adam sat with them, talking about Adam's plans for the future and his and Nan's work in the library. Nan finally went into the kitchen and made hot chocolate for them. When she came back into the living room, Adam was alone. "Your parents said to say good night."

They stared at each other, and then Adam took the two mugs from her and held her in his arms. He kissed her gently and then with more feeling. "I love you, Nan," he said.

Nan moved away from him. Reality had returned abruptly. "My boyfriend is coming home next weekend, Adam. Nothing is different for you and me."

Adam kissed her again, and she didn't resist. "I doubt that," he said softly. He pushed back the hair from her forehead and smiled. "Whoever thought fairy princesses should be blond was a very unimaginative person."

After they finished their hot chocolates, Adam put on his jacket and walked to the door. "See you in school Monday," he said.

Nan nodded and then put her arms around him. "Adam. Adam, it was the most perfect evening of my life." She kissed him deeply, and he left.

Nan went back into the living room and sank down onto the couch. Tears ran down her face, and she took a throw pillow and clutched it to her. Her mind was filled with a confusion of thoughts about Adam and Mac and love and friendship. And what she felt for each of the boys and why. She tried to sort the feelings out, but she was too tired to make any sense of them. She walked slowly into her bedroom, feeling happier and sadder and more confused than she ever had.

Chapter Thirteen

Nan wondered how Adam would react to her during the next week. She was afraid he might pressure her to go out with him again, but he didn't. He was friendly, nice, funny, but he didn't refer to Friday night at all. Yet, whenever Nan glanced at him, he was looking at her in a way that was different from before.

And Nan tried her best to treat Adam just like any other boy. She didn't talk to him or look at him any more than usual. But that wonderful snowy night was as magical in her thoughts as it had been in reality.

By the time Mac came home the next Friday, most of the snowdrifts had been carted away by the sanitation men. Along the curbs only, small banks of blackened snow remained to remind Nan of her night with Adam.

When Mac rang the Whitmans' bell Friday evening, Nan opened the door and reached out for him. He held her in his arms, and she let the tensions and concerns of the week melt away. She was back in the familiar warmth of Mac's arms, and that was where she wanted to be. They sat in Nan's living room and talked very little. Mac kissed her and held her, and they both relaxed in their ease with each other.

The next day they went to three museums, ate hot dogs from a stand, had dinner at a Greek restaurant, and finally returned to Nan's apartment. The day had been pleasant, but strained. What puzzled Nan was that she knew the strain was coming not only from *her* feelings of confusion about what she felt for Mac, but something was coming from *him*, too.

When they finally were sitting on the couch in the living room, Nan wasn't sure what to talk about with him. She started three different conversations, only to let them drift off. Mac stood up and walked up and down the room, looking at books and paintings on the walls as if he had never seen them before. Then he sat down next to Nan again and put his arm around her. She put her head down on his shoulder and tried to feel as if Adam didn't exist. But she knew he did. At the same time she felt love and warmth for Mac, too, but a different kind from what she felt for Adam.

"I love you, Nannie," Mac said softly.

Nan heard a tone in his voice she had never heard when he had said those very words in the past.

"But?"

"What do you mean?" Mac said.

"It's the tone." Nan buried her face deeper in his shoulder. "It's an I-love-you-but tone."

Mac cleared his throat. "We've made a mistake, Nannie."

In spite of herself, Nan felt cold. "What kind of mistake?"

Mac went on. "We never should have decided not to go out with other people. It doesn't make sense when we're so far apart." He held her closer. "This doesn't mean I don't care about you."

Suddenly Nan realized something. She sat upright and looked at Mac. "It's a girl, isn't it? I mean, one special girl you've met that you want to date. Isn't that it?"

Mac looked pale. "In a way." He paused for a moment, thoughtful. "I haven't been really going out with her, Nan. I met her at a couple of parties, and I'd like to see her again. I love you, Nan. I do, but—"

Nan started to laugh.

"What's so darn funny?"

She put her hand over his. "It's OK, Mac. It really is—because the same thing happened to me."

"You met a guy you want to go out with?"

Nan nodded. "I can't believe that both of us are in the same boat."

Mac smiled slightly. "It's funny, I'm the one who brought this up, and yet I'm a little jealous."

Nan smiled, too. "I know. What's she like?"

Mac took Nan's hand and kept gazing at it. "She's a lot like you. Smart and funny and easy to talk to. What's *he* like?"

Nan sighed. "He's a lot like you, too."

Then they were clinging to each other, and tears came to Nan's eyes.

"I'll always love you, Nan. Maybe not like we've been loving each other, but you'll always be important to me," Mac said.

"I feel the same way," she said. "I'll always care about you in a special way."

Mac held her tightly. "I'll still call you and write and see you when I come home."

Nan laughed. "Well, I won't count on the writing."

Then Mac stood up. "I have to go. I have a really early flight tomorrow."

She walked him to the door, and once again they clung to each other. "I'll talk to you soon," he said. Then he kissed her very gently. "Goodbye, Nan," he said, and then he left.

Nan went into her bedroom, changed into her nightgown, and got into bed. She lay there hardly moving. She felt stranger than she ever had. There was an excitement about not being Mac's girlfriend, a freedom she had never had before. Now she would be able to see Adam openly and honestly and as much as she wanted. But with the feeling of freedom, there was also a feeling of great loss. A part of her life, a part that had been supportive and constant, was gone. She knew she was moving to a different place in her life, and it frightened her. She huddled deeper under the covers and waited to feel warmer; she was so cold. She got up and walked to Zoe's room.

There were twin beds in Zoe's bedroom so that visiting relatives and friends always had a place to sleep. Nan went in, pulled down the spread on the empty bed, and got under the covers. She heard Zoe's quiet, even breathing and began to feel herself relax. The coldness began to leave her body.

Then Zoe sat up in bed and snapped on the light. They both blinked in the sudden brightness.

"How come you're in here?" Zoe asked, squinting at Nan.

"I just felt like it. I didn't feel like sleeping alone."

Zoe looked at Nan for a moment. "How come?" she asked again.

I don't want to talk about it now, Nan thought. *I just want her to let me be.* Aloud she said, "I'll tell you in the morning."

Zoe stared at Nan. "OK," she said. "Go to sleep." She turned off the light and slipped down under the covers.

When Nan woke up in the morning, Zoe was sitting up, watching her. "How come? You said you'd tell me in the morning."

Briefly, Nan told her what had happened. "Please don't say anything to Mom and Dad yet. I want to get used to it myself."

Zoe agreed. "Now you can see Adam. Right? And maybe you won't look so sad most of the time."

"I have to think about all of this. I still feel very funny."

Zoe got out of bed. "I'm hungry. See you later."

Nan wandered around the apartment aimlessly for most of the day. She wanted to call Adam, but something kept stopping her.

There seemed to be something so ludicrous about running from Mac right to Adam.

She spoke to Wendy during the day, and Wendy said, in her usual direct way, "Oh, stop wasting time. Call him!"

At three-thirty Nan took a deep breath, looked up Adam's phone number, and dialed.

When he answered, she asked, "How would you like me to take you out for a hamburger tonight?"

Nan sensed Adam's unasked questions. He hesitated and then answered. "Sure. But you'd better realize I'm not a cheap date. I go for bacon, cheese, tomatoes—the works. French fries, too."

Nan let her breath out softly. "I'll go for broke this time."

"Nan," Adam said. "Oh, Nan." Then, "I'll pick you up at six."

After she hung up, Nan sat quietly for a few minutes. She thought about everything that had happened since she first began helping out at the library—the friends she had made, Adam. Then she went into Zoe's room.

"You were right," she said.

"I was?" Zoe asked in surprise.

Nan nodded. "You said I should do something I liked, for a change. When I did, things

141

happened that I couldn't make happen before."

"I told you I was wise beyond my years." Zoe ducked as Nan threw a pillow at her.

"I did something else I liked, too. I called Adam, and I'm taking him out for a hamburger tonight."

Zoe looked distressed. "Just make sure he's worth it before you spend a fortune on him. You can buy *me* a hamburger, if you're just in a buying mood."

"I think he's worth it," Nan answered. "I'm willing to take a chance and just see what happens naturally."

"Good," Zoe said. "You're learning." She ducked again as another pillow sailed over her head.

Her mom and dad were in the living room reading the Sunday papers when Nan walked in.

"I won't be home for dinner tonight. I'm going out for a hamburger with Adam."

Mrs. Whitman raised her eyebrows and exchanged a look with her husband. "Oh? I didn't hear the phone ring."

Nan sat on the floor and hugged her knees. "It didn't. I called him. I'm taking *him* out."

Mr. Whitman sighed. "I was born in the

wrong time. No pretty girl ever took me out for dinner."

Nan smiled at him, then turned to her mother. "Mom, take him out sometime."

"Do you have enough money?" her dad asked.

Nan counted in her head. "Just about."

Her father walked over to her, reached into his pocket, and took out a bill. He slipped it into Nan's hand, saying, "Take this. Never let it be said my daughter doesn't know how to take a guy out."

Nan dressed carefully that night, putting on good jeans and a pale green turtleneck sweater that emphasized her dark hair and the brown in her eyes. She pulled her hair back with two combs, wanting to look as different as she was feeling. She added soft eye makeup and some lip gloss, then looked at herself in the mirror. "What's ahead for you, Nan Whitman?" she asked her reflection.

She tried to read while she waited for Adam, but she couldn't concentrate. She walked over to her bureau and picked up the picture of Mac. He was smiling at her, and she smiled back. She felt close to him, but knew that the romantic love they had felt for each other for years was gone. In its place was a peaceful, warm feeling that she hoped she would always have about him.

When she heard the bell ring, she ran to the door. Adam's cheeks were pink from the cold, and his hair was windblown. He reached up and nervously straightened it.

"Let's not hang around here," Nan said. "I'd like to go right now."

"Sure," Adam said.

Nan grabbed her down jacket from the closet near the door and yelled in to her parents, who were in the living room. "We're going. See you later."

Adam reached his hand out and held Nan back. "Wait."

He walked to the living room and waved at the Whitmans. "Hi."

They waved at him, and Adam went back to Nan. "It's always good to have a girl's parents think you're a nice guy."

Nan laughed and looked at him with surprise. "You're a schemer, and I never knew it."

They walked to a nearby hamburger place, not talking but holding hands tightly. The air was crisp and cold, and Nan pulled the collar of her jacket up around her neck.

In the restaurant the waitress came over and handed a menu to each of them. Adam read his carefully and finally decided.

"You first," he said to Nan.

"A cheeseburger, french fries, and a milkshake," she said to the waitress.

"You?" the waitress said, looking at Adam.

Adam dramatically took a deep breath. "OK. Cheeseburger with bacon, tomatoes, lettuce, pickle, french fries, and a shake. Oh, yeah, and raw onions on it, too."

The waitress looked at him and then at Nan. "Sure about the onions?"

"Sure," Adam answered.

The waitress looked back at Nan. "Poor thing. You must really like him to put up with raw onions."

When the woman left, Nan and Adam were silent. Nan knew he was waiting for her to say something about why she had called him.

Nan pushed the silverware on the table around in circles. "Mac was here for the weekend. You know that. Well, we decided that we made a mistake, not seeing other people. So we agreed that we should be free to date."

Adam was looking at her carefully. "How do you feel about him? Is he still your boyfriend?"

Nan hesitated. The discussion was much harder than she had thought it would be because Adam always asked such direct questions.

"I guess he's not a 'boyfriend' in the

romantic sense anymore. He's a boy and he's my friend—a very good friend. And I'm still going to write and talk to him on the phone and see him when he comes home, but—it's different."

Adam persisted. "Is that OK with you?"

Nan nodded and answered in a whisper, "Yes."

"Is that OK with him?"

Nan nodded again.

"What do you want to do about us?" Adam asked.

Nan moved in her seat nervously. "Why do *I* have to answer all these questions? What do you want to do about us?"

Adam reached out and took her hand. "I'm sorry. I just want to make sure we're both feeling the same way. I like you an awful lot. I want us to see a lot of each other and really get to know each other."

Nan looked at his hand on top of hers. The fingers were long, with square nails. She squeezed his hand. "I want that, too, but—"

"But?"

Nan took a deep breath."I don't want us to only see each other or anything like that. I mean, I really like you tremendously, but you're going to college in the fall, and I don't want to be in the same place I was with Mac. I don't want us to make promises we won't be able to keep."

Adam took his hand away but kept looking in Nan's eyes. "That's OK with me. I don't want us to get into the mess you were in with Mac, either. But there's no other girl I want to see now."

Nan smiled. "There's no other guy *I* want to see now."

They grabbed each other's hands again. Adam let out his breath in a great rush. "Wow. Look at us. We're together, and we can be together as much as we want. What could be better?"

The waitress came to the table and put their food in front of them. She watched as Adam put mounds of ketchup on his french fries. Then he looked at the woman and back at Nan. Carefully, he removed the raw onions from his hamburger and put them on the side. The waitress nodded at him approvingly. "Much better," she said.

"Well," he said, "just in case."

The strain was gone, and they ate and talked and laughed. They ordered one huge sundae and shared it, licking the whipped cream off each other's spoons.

When Adam walked her home, they stopped in front of her apartment house. "I won't come up tonight," he said. "I don't want to talk to anyone but you."

He put his hands on Nan's shoulders and kissed her gently. "See you tomorrow."

When she got upstairs, Nan went straight to her room, got ready for bed, and fell asleep immediately. She was worn out by the events of the weekend but felt a peace she hadn't felt for months.

Chapter Fourteen

The next day when she got to her first class, Adam was waiting for her. "Are you busy Friday night?"

Nan felt a lovely warmth spread through her. "No. Are you?"

Adam took her hand for a moment and then let it go. "Nope. Let's do something special, to celebrate the beginning of something wonderful."

In the library that afternoon, Joyce Unger sensed immediately that something was different between Nan and Adam. "What's happening to you two?" she asked.

Nan told her briefly.

"Good," Joyce said. "It makes much more sense that way. And you'll both get a lot more work done, which will be great with me."

The week sped by. Nan and Adam saw each other every day in the library, and once or twice they stopped for Cokes before they went home. She told her parents what Mac and she had decided and knew they were both a little relieved.

On Thursday in the library, Adam said to Nan, "Do you remember what you wore the night of the blizzard?"

"A red nose," she said.

"That's true, but besides that—what else?"

Nan thought for a moment. "Jeans and my red sweater."

"Wear that again tomorrow."

"Where are we going?" Nan asked.

Adam smiled. "It's a surprise."

They stayed in the library the next day until after five. When they left school, Adam took Nan's hand, and they walked through the cold streets. "Where are we going?" she asked again.

"Back to the Italian restaurant we went to that night. OK?"

"Sure." She smiled. "You're a romantic, Adam. And sentimental, too."

He nodded. "A little."

In the restaurant Adam asked for the same table they had sat at before. A fire crackled in the fireplace, and Nan sat at the table, feeling warm inside and out. Soon the same palm reader appeared and walked right over to them.

"May I read your hand?" she asked Nan.

"I don't think so. Remember, you read it once?"

The palmist said, "I remember."

Adam pulled a chair from another table over to theirs. "This time I have enough money. Read her palm again."

The woman sat down and took Nan's hand. She looked at it carefully in silence and then spoke. "There is a difference from the last time. Yes, there is."

"What kind of difference?" Nan leaned toward her eagerly.

"I see a big change in your life and a boy who likes you a lot. There is also a boy next door who is now a friend, but this new boy is some-one special to you. I see a lot of books and you with this new boy. He cares about you a great deal, and you will have many happy times with him for many years to come. You are not to be afraid, for even when he goes away, he will care about you."

The woman traced a line in Nan's hand. "I see great success for you in whatever you do and riches, too. Oh, yes, you will travel to far places, and you will be happy. Just like I said last time."

Adam paid her, and she left the table. Nan burst out laughing. "You arranged that, didn't you? You set it all up."

"Well—yes, I did."

"How did you do it?" Nan asked softly.

"I stopped by here a couple of days ago and asked her if she would play cupid. She didn't mind at all."

Nan leaned toward him. "You are special, Adam, and fun, and you do wonderful things."

Adam took her hand. "What she said was true. I do care about you a lot, and we will have happy times, and I love you, Nan."

Nan reached over and touched his cheek. "I love you, too."

After dinner they sat in a small park in a busy square and huddled together against the cold. Adam put his arm around Nan. "It would have been perfect if it had snowed, too, but I guess you can't have everything."

"We have an awful lot, Adam." Nan shifted on the bench. "Will you do me a favor?"

"Name it."

"The next time you talk to our palmist, will you ask her where I'm going to travel to?"

"Sure. But I can guess. I'm going to school

in New Haven, so let's say Connecticut will be first on your list."

"That wasn't quite what I had in mind. But you know, if you're there, Connecticut will be almost as good as Paris."

They sat in silence, each going over the unexpected and wonderful thing that had happened to them.

Thank you, Zoe, Nan thought. *Doing what you like can't be beat.*

☐	23969-4	**DOUBLE LOVE #1** Francine Pascal	$2.25
☐	23971	**SECRETS #2** Francine Pascal	$2.25
☐	23972	**PLAYING WITH FIRE #3** Francine Pascal	$2.25
☐	23730	**POWER PLAY #4** Francine Pascal	$2.25
☐	23943	**ALL NIGHT LONG #5** Francine Pascal	$2.25
☐	23938	**DANGEROUS LOVE #6** Francine Pascal	$2.25
☐	24001	**DEAR SISTER #7** Francine Pascal	$2.25
☐	24045	**HEARTBREAKER #8** Francine Pascal	$2.25
☐	24131	**RACING HEARTS #9** Francine Pascal	$2.25
☐	24182	**WRONG KIND OF GIRL #10** Francine Pascal	$2.25
☐	24252	**TOO GOOD TO BE TRUE #11** Francine Pascal	$2.25

Prices and availability subject to change without notice.

Buy them at your local bookstore or use this handy coupon for ordering: